"What more could you want than to have this every day?"

"I don't know," Jack said, his voice a mere whisper, and when she turned to him, the look on his face took her aback. His expression was tight, his eyes narrowed on the world below. "When I leave, that's the first thing I plan to find out."

There was such an emptiness in his tone that it made Jillian move back half a pace. She didn't want to feel the loneliness in this man. She didn't want to have an impulse to touch him, to make contact in some way. She didn't want that at all. And that made her turn abruptly and say words that sounded hollow to her as they hung in the air between them. "I hope it works for you."

At least that was better than sharing her own pain and blurting out the truth.

That she was not what she seemed. That this was all a lie.

Dear Reader,

In *Jack and Jillian*, the fourth book in my RETURN TO SILVER CREEK series, Jack Prescott, a man who owns most of the town of Silver Creek, Nevada, watches his closest friends fall in love, and when he looks at his own life, he knows it's not what he wants. He can't even remember what his dreams were for his life.

Jack Prescott is leaving Silver Creek to find his future, whatever it may be. Jillian O'Shay knows what her life is, and that any dreams she had were pushed aside to live it. When she visits Silver Creek on a job assignment, she meets Jack and they both realize that sometimes the life you've been searching for—the life you've only dreamed of having—comes to you where and when you least expect it.

I hope you enjoy the journey of Jack and Jillian as they find their dreams and their future with each other in Silver Creek.

Jack and Jillian

Mary Anne Wilson

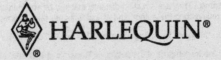

HARLEQUIN®

TORONTO • NEW YORK • LONDON
AMSTERDAM • PARIS • SYDNEY • HAMBURG
STOCKHOLM • ATHENS • TOKYO • MILAN • MADRID
PRAGUE • WARSAW • BUDAPEST • AUCKLAND

ISBN 0-373-75109-5

JACK AND JILLIAN

www.eHarlequin.com

Printed in U.S.A.

For Tom
For being there to hold my
hand when I needed it.
I love you.

Books by Mary Anne Wilson

HARLEQUIN AMERICAN ROMANCE

1003—PREDICTING RAIN?*
1005—WINNING SARA'S HEART*
1009—WHEN MEGAN SMILES*
1062—DISCOVERING DUNCAN†
1078—JUDGING JOSHUA†
1092—HOLIDAY HOMECOMING†

*Just for Kids
†Return to Silver Creek

Prologue

San Francisco

Jillian O'Shay felt very alone, even though there were two other people in the cheerful bedroom of the four-story, renovated Victorian home that sat on the fringes of the Nob Hill district. The nurse, May Reynolds, a tall, smiling, buxom woman who'd been at the Sunshine Care facility since its opening five years before, was helping Jillian's father, Johnny, put a blanket over his knees in the wheelchair.

At last she patted him on the shoulder. "There you go, Mr. O'Shay. You've got yourself a real pretty view from here."

Johnny stared straight ahead as if studying the view through the closed French doors, but Jillian knew that her father wasn't taking in the second-story balcony lined with flowers in pots outside the doors, or the narrow glimpse of the bay, choppy and gray on that December day.

Johnny didn't take in much of anything anymore. Except for the wheelchair, he looked like any sixty-four-year-old man might look. He had a shock of white hair, crow's-feet around brilliant blue eyes and large, capable-looking hands. His strong jaw was freshly shaven.

"Dad, it's going to be nice here." Jillian moved closer and touched his left hand. His skin was cool. "I'll be around a lot, and if you need anything, they'll let me know. When I'm working, they can contact Ray and he'll know what to do."

Johnny didn't move for a long moment, then finally turned his eyes on Jillian. He studied her, then a smile came, an expression her mother had always said could charm the birds out of the trees.

"Hello," he said in a voice rough from disuse.

She hunkered down beside him and smiled back. "Hello, Dad."

His smile faltered and he frowned at her. "Dad? Why did you call me that? Do I know you?"

Jillian had known it would come. It had been like this for the past three months. He usually didn't know her, but that didn't soften the impact on her. "I'm Jillian, your daughter," she said, then watched him turn away from her, the frown gone and his gaze on the closed French doors.

She slowly stood up, and May put a hand on her shoulder. "Sweetie, he'll have good days," she said. "But he'll have bad days. Moving is always a huge thing for Alzheimer's patients. They need sameness and a sense of home. That's what he'll find here."

Jillian bit her lip hard, then murmured a thanks. Needing to get out of that room, she headed for the door. She stepped out into the hallway, closed the door quietly behind her, then stopped and leaned one shoulder against the wood-lined wall. Closing her eyes, she willed herself to be calm.

This was her decision. Hers alone. She'd done what she'd had to do. It was that simple. With her job and all the traveling she did, a nursing home for Dad was her only option. Quitting her job was not. She needed all the money she could make to keep Johnny safe.

She opened her eyes and straightened, then tugged at the cuffs of her old UCB sweatshirt she wore with faded jeans and jogging shoes. Her pale, strawberry-blond hair was pulled back in a ponytail. As tiny as Johnny was big, she was five foot three and weighed 110 pounds—eight inches shorter than her dad and a hundred pounds lighter. She did, however, have her father's blue eyes and his Irish stubbornness.

"Jillian?"

She turned at the sound of her name and was so relieved to see Cameron James coming down the hallway toward her she could have cried. She'd had dates who had never called again after meeting her father. Cameron *had* called again, and for the past month, while she'd been making the arrangements to have Johnny moved here, had seen her at least once a week. His presence had helped a lot.

"Is the move done?" Cameron asked abruptly, and she felt her pleasure at his appearance start to fade.

"He's settling in," she said, wrapping her arms around her middle.

"Good, good." He reached her and kissed her cheek lightly. "Then let's go and get some coffee and figure out what we're going to do this weekend."

Cameron was half a foot taller than she, with dark, razor-cut hair, a clean-shaven jaw and a penchant for three-piece suits. On their first date he'd told her that he was on the fast track in the brokerage house where he worked, and that within a year he intended to be their most influential stockbroker. In five years he saw himself with his own brokerage. Now, in his charcoal-gray suit and polished, wing-tipped shoes, he looked every bit the successful broker.

"I can't leave yet," she said.

He frowned. "You're paying a fortune for them to take care of him. Let them earn their pay."

His words were like knives. She stared at Cameron. "But I'm his daughter. He needs to know I'm here."

Cameron lowered his voice. "He doesn't know anyone, not even you. He won't know where he is, and he won't know if you're here or not."

Whatever she'd let herself believe about where things could go with Cameron, she'd been wrong. Oddly, she didn't feel particularly hurt. It was almost as if she'd been expecting the moment when she knew she wouldn't see him anymore. "I'm staying."

His frown deepened, then Cameron checked his expensive wristwatch. "Okay, that's your choice, but I have an appointment in an hour." His brown eyes met hers. "I thought we could talk, but…" He shrugged. "I guess not."

"No," she said. "I guess not."

Then he acted as if nothing had happened. "Okay, catch you later, babe," he said, then gave her another peck on her cheek and left.

She watched him hurry off and out of sight down the stairs. His world was right. Hers was not. And he would never be part of her world. She stood straighter, swiped at her eyes, then took a deep breath before going back into Johnny's room. This was her world. This was what she had to deal with. And she'd do it the way she had for the past seven years—alone.

Chapter One

Silver Creek, Nevada
Three years later

Jack Prescott looked around the suite he lived in at The Inn at Silver Creek and faced a basic fact in his life. He had everything. He had enough money to do anything he wanted. He had a handful of close, really good friends, and he had this resort he'd built from the ground up. His accountant had once told him that if he spent money every waking hour for the rest of his life, he'd die rich. Then they'd both laughed. He wasn't laughing now. His wealth didn't matter. Nothing mattered anymore.

He raked a hand through his dark brown hair, flecked with gray, and exhaled on a rough sigh. When had everything stopped mattering? God, he wished he knew. At thirty-eight, he should have had the world by the tail. Instead, he felt as if the world had him. He crossed the shadowed suite, poured a drink then sank into one of two leather couches and stared at the fire in the stone hearth.

He took a long swallow of whiskey, let the fire burn through him, then he eased low in the supple pillows and stretched his booted feet out in front of him. He was here, and he didn't want to be here. Yet he wasn't sure where he *did* want to be. All he knew was, he wanted to wake up in the morning and be excited about another day. He couldn't remember when that had last happened, but he remembered when he'd realized he'd lost the ability to be excited.

He'd managed to get a hold of a chunk of land he'd wanted to incorporate into the grounds of The Inn for years. It had the best skiing imaginable, and it butted up against the north end of The Inn's property. It had been a self-imposed test for him: get the land and everything would be right; get the land and nothing would be right.

So he'd gone after the land, focused on it—and then he'd gotten it. The land had fallen into his lap with an ease that had been startling.

And that was when he knew. At that moment nothing had been right. Nothing mattered.

That was when he'd made the final decision to leave Silver Creek. He'd secure things here at The Inn, maybe sell off some of his holdings, including the new acquisition, which didn't mean a thing to him now, and he'd walk out the door. He'd go, and keep going until that one morning when he'd awaken and he'd be excited about the new day. That was when he'd know he'd found what he was looking for.

He finished off his drink, then stood and headed into

his bedroom. He stepped out of his boots, stripped off his chambray shirt and jeans, and fell onto the cool linen on his huge, four-poster bed. He stretched out on his back and stared into the deep shadows that surrounded him. In a week, two weeks tops, he'd go.

As he settled that, a huge weight seemed to lift off him and he rolled onto his side. It was his life, and he'd make it what he wanted it to be. Whatever that turned out to be. He'd do it, and he'd do it alone, the way he'd pretty much done everything in his life.

IT WAS LATE December, just a couple of days to the new year, and Jillian was working. She'd worked most holidays in the past few years, usually thankful for the distraction of work. Christmas this year had been empty for her, alone in her apartment, then spending an hour at the care facility with Johnny. But over the New Year's holiday, she'd work and make the money she needed. But for some reason, as she drove into the small skiing town of Silver Creek, she felt vaguely depressed at what her life had become.

Self-pity wasn't something she ever indulged in and she wouldn't start now. She was on her way to one of the most exclusive resorts in the country, so that wasn't all bad. She'd be paid to stay there for a week, and all she had to do was take notice of what made The Inn at Silver Creek so desirable and exclusive. "A piece of cake," she muttered, and paid attention to her driving.

The snow that had been falling ever since she'd

started her climb into the Sierra Nevada Mountains had finally stopped. Plows were busy clearing the main street in the town, and traffic backed up behind the lumbering machinery. She didn't mind. It gave her a few extra moments to take in her surroundings.

The valley slashed through the mountains, rugged peaks that disappeared into dark clouds on the west and east sides. Whoever had laid out the town had taken the path of least resistance, which had resulted in a route that gave visitors a view of the scenery that was awe-inspiring.

Silver Creek was a nice little town. It had a perfect location in the mountain range that ridged between California and Nevada. It was the right size, not overly large, not too small, and easily accessible from Las Vegas or from northern California. A nice little package.

The main street wandered north and south in the natural cut, with side streets fanning out and up into the foothills. Skiers were everywhere, taking their time crossing the streets, going from one specialty shop to another, housed in the two- and three-story brick buildings that lined the way. Many held cups of hot coffee or chocolate in their hands, the steam from which mingled in the frigid air with their exhaled breaths. Cars filled every space set aside for parking, and the lights from the businesses flashed with every imaginable color.

Although she was driving the luxury SUV she had rented in Las Vegas at a pace that would rival a snail's, she felt the back tires lose traction for a moment when she braked. Almost immediately, the car was stable again, and she realized she was at the end of a long line of cars waiting to get into the parking lot for the public lifts. An attendant bundled in heavy clothes came walking down the line, stopping at each car, saying something, then moving on.

He reached her car, and as she slid down the window, he said quickly, "Only got B parking, in the satellite lot. Twenty dollars for the day, and two by the hour."

"I just want to get past," she said, her breathing clouding into the frigid air.

He motioned her to the right. "Go around the car in front of you, and there's enough room for you to keep going."

"Thanks," she said. She put up the window and did as he said. In less than a minute, she was past the long line and heading out of the main town. The last of the businesses fell away, and a scattering of houses could be seen well back from the road.

As she headed out of town on a narrow two-lane highway, climbing higher into the mountains, the phone in the console rang. Only one person had this number, so it wasn't a stretch for her to answer it with "Hi, Ray."

"Hello there," her boss, Ray Shelley, said cheerfully.

Jill had a vivid mental image of the stocky man back in San Francisco, sitting in his ridiculously huge leather chair in his overdone office, running a hand over his almost bald head and frowning intently. An ever-present cigar would be haloing smoke over him, despite the no-smoking signs everywhere. "I'm on my way out the door for a party," he said, "but I wanted to check and make sure you're all in place."

"I just passed through Silver Creek and I'm heading to The Inn," she murmured.

"Great. I'm also calling to let you know that Prescott is going to be at The Inn for a week after New Year's, but not much longer."

Jack Prescott, the man who literally built The Inn at Silver Creek from the ground up, was going to be there when she got to The Inn. That could be a good thing. "Well, your spies have been busy little beavers, haven't they?" she murmured as she eyed the great mounds of snow that plows had deposited on both sides of the highway.

"You're the only spy I have anywhere near The Inn at the moment."

She frowned at the term "spy," but she realized that her job really didn't have an easy title. She observed businesses, analyzed their operations and wrote reports for her client, whoever that was at the time. Sure, she did it anonymously, blending in any way she could to get the information she needed to get, but *spy* wasn't a word she liked to use. She got her assignments through Ray and his Platinum Group's development division, and if anyone asked, she'd say she was an evaluator. They didn't know what that meant, but so far, no one had asked her to elaborate.

"Then how do you know Prescott's going to be there

when I arrive? The last I heard no one knew if he'd be there at all."

"He called Dennis Wright, our head attorney, and said he'd heard through *his* channels that we might be brokering a deal for one of his holdings. He wanted to verify it."

"And what was he told?"

"Wright told him the truth."

She involuntarily slowed the car at this admission and got a sharp retort from the horn of a car behind her. She sped up and said, "Everything?"

"No, of course not. Just what he needed to know."

She exhaled. "Okay, tell me what he was told. I don't want to get tripped up while I'm there, especially if he's in the vicinity and there's any chance of my meeting him."

Ray said that the attorney had verified that they were "considering" being a broker for some land in that area. As she listened, the impatient car behind her cut out into the oncoming lane to pass her. It was a fire-engine-red Porsche and it roared alongside her, so close she felt the SUV almost shudder; then the driver gunned the engine and cut back into the lane right in front of her.

The Porsche went even faster now, disappearing around a curve ahead, and she fully expected to hear screeching brakes and a crash. She didn't, but at least the car was gone, and she slowed again. "And he didn't ask any more questions?" she finally said when Ray paused.

"I don't know, but I'm sure Wright used the old 'I'm

not at liberty to say.' I suspect Prescott has people digging into it right now. He'll find out that Platinum is considering a number of properties in the area. His is just one of them."

That wasn't what she'd been told. Their client wanted Prescott's property, period. "So he's selling for sure?"

"I don't know. He recently acquired the land our client wants, but his people sent out the word that he was considering turning over some of his assets, that land included—if things go right and if he likes what's brought to him." Ray released a hiss of air over the line. "He seems in a hurry to leave Silver Creek and I figure he wants to streamline his holdings. It's just not easy dealing with a man who is so personally involved in every business decision, even when he's letting go of some holdings."

People who owned most of any town seldom let go of it. A large chunk of Silver Creek belonged to Prescott. He'd be a fool to throw away his holdings, and from what Jill knew of the man, he wasn't a fool. She spotted a high fence all but covered with the snow off to the left. It ran north as far as she could see. "Then this is all on speculation until he decides?"

"And until our client decides if they can do what they think they can with that land," Ray said.

The entrance for The Inn came into view. She saw a large area of cobbled drive to the left, the space totally devoid of snow. Set well back from the road was a set of intricately carved wooden gates, tall enough to hide whatever was beyond them. She turned across the highway onto the rough cobble of the drive, and before she had time to even wonder how she'd get inside, a guard emerged from a small side building and hurried toward her.

"Hold on," she said into the phone to Ray as the guard got close, and she pressed the satellite phone to her jade-green designer jacket. She hit the button for the window and felt a blast of frigid air invade the climate-controlled interior.

"Welcome to The Inn," the guard, a pleasant-looking, middle-aged man, said as he bent slightly to look at her.

"I'm Jillian O'Shay and—"

He smiled quickly. "Oh, yes, Miss O'Shay, we're expecting you." He motioned ahead of her. "Straight through there, up to the main building, and Morris will be at the portico to help you with your car and luggage."

"Thanks," she said, and put the window back up. In moments, the gates swung back to let her pass. She drove between the massive stone pillars and onto the grounds of The Inn at Silver Creek. One of the best ski resorts in the country. Private, luxurious, everything someone who had the money to spend demanded.

She heard a muffled sound and remembered Ray on the phone. "Hey, sorry," she murmured as her gaze skimmed over the view in front of her and up the sweep of the cobbled drive, lined by towering banks of snow. "The guard was letting me in."

"You're on the grounds?"

"Sure am," she breathed as she drove toward the main lodge, a huge meandering building that changed in spots from three stories to one, then two and back to three. She knew it had more than sixty private guest rooms, and so much more. "This looks a lot different than it does in photos."

"Better?"

That was an understatement. "Much better." She kept speaking into the phone as she approached the main lodge. "It's rustic, all stone and wood, fits right in with the landscape. Perfect location." She let out a soft, low whistle. "There are stained-glass windows, stone chimneys and a sweep of protected area under a jutting portico." She slowed as she approached that portico. It took her a minute to realize that the men she saw in ski sweaters and boots weren't guests, but valets and door people. "No uniforms at all so far. Informal clothing, but obviously expensive clothing."

"Rustic, you said?"

"Yeah, but a rich version of it," she replied as she took in the main entryway. The dark wooden doors had to be twenty feet high and each was probably six feet wide. Stone stairs lined with potted pines swept up to them. Each meticulously maintained pine was laced with soft lights that twinkled in the failing light of the late afternoon. She hadn't even come to a full stop before a valet was there, opening her door and letting in a blast of icy air.

"I'll be in touch," Ray said. "Just leave a message and I'll get back to you."

"Can you check on Dad every once in a while?"

"No problem. They've got my number, so don't worry."

Easier said than done, she thought, but said, "I'll get pictures," then flipped off the phone.

"Miss O'Shay, I'm Morris." The attendant held out his hand. "I'll get you inside where it's warm, then I'll see to your car and luggage."

She let him help her out of the car and said, "I'll find my own way inside."

"Of course," he said agreeably. Obviously whatever the guest wanted, the guest got. No questions asked. She reached back for her leather shoulder bag, the satellite phone and her laptop. When she turned, Morris was still there, smiling at her. "James will meet you inside to show you to your room."

"Thanks," she said and ducked past the man to head for the entry steps. As she passed the trees on the stone steps, the scent of pine met her nostrils, along with the fragrance of wood smoke. She approached the doors, and the right one opened the moment she neared it. Another attendant in another ski outfit greeted her. He introduced himself as James, then quickly took her computer case and led her across a massive central room.

She didn't know if the space would be labeled a reception area or a meeting room or a lounge. It seemed to be all three. The ceiling was soaring and fashioned with heavy beams. An impressive stone fireplace stood in the center, decorated with leather and a few animal hides, along with brass used for emphasis. The fire was going, and people lounged in the overstuffed chairs, some in conversation, some sipping drinks by the fire and some just sitting. One man sat in a lounge sipping brandy, one leg in a heavy cast.

James took her through the room toward the back, where she expected to see a check-in desk, but instead, there was an alcove with a series of tables that probably acted as desks. A girl, dressed not unlike the other attendants, was sitting at one of the tables, and when she saw Jillian, she stood up and smiled at her. "Hello, Ms. O'Shay, welcome to The Inn." Hmm, Jillian thought. There must be a radio system from the gate to the lodge. The woman, a tiny person with dark hair and big dark eyes, looked toward James. She gave him a room number, then held out a security key card to Jillian. "If you need more, just ask. Meanwhile, James will see you to your suite, and please, call me if you need anything at all. My name is Brenda."

"Thanks, Brenda," Jillian murmured, then went with James through one of three stone archways cut into the walls.

She thought they took the middle one, but she could have been wrong. She'd check later. She knew they were going into the north wing of the lodge. They passed a few shops, one that displayed the most astounding jewelry, then what looked like a restaurant and coffee bar. Finally they reached the elevators.

James pressed the call button, and when the car came, he stood back for her to enter, then he followed and they headed up to the third floor. James started to give what she assumed was the usual talk about The Inn. "This building, the lodge, is fully equipped for any of your needs." He smiled at her. "Anything at all. Nothing is too big or too small. There are restaurants, bars, sitting areas, a wonderful spa, designer clothes at the Top of the Mark shop, and trinkets at the jewelers. If we don't have it here, we can bring it in. Anything you wish."

The elevator stopped as she murmured, "That's good to know," and he let her step out first.

The hallway was hushed, decorated with Persian carpets, polished cherrywood walls, an arched stone ceiling and wonderful art pieces. "This way," James said, and led her to the left, to a curve in the hallway and to a door at the end of the passage. He opened it, stood back and let her step inside.

She'd been in luxury hotels all over the world, but this one stopped her for a moment. There was an outer room, a place to sit and visit by a fireplace, in chairs of supple leather. A wide adjoining hallway was lined on both sides by closed doors—probably walk-in closets. She saw her bags sitting by the nearest door. She was impressed. She didn't know how they'd been able to get the bags up here so quickly.

She moved down the hallway and into the main room of the suite. Calling it a bedroom would have been too simple. It had two levels, one for the bed and one for a full entertainment center with a big-screen television set built into the wall, a sitting area and a bank of doors that opened to what she guessed was a balcony. All she could see beyond the windows was a stone railing.

It wasn't only the sheer luxury that struck her, but the obvious thought put into even the tiniest detail. The staff seemed impeccable, not gushing with phoney platitudes. They just did their jobs and did them well, without drawing attention to themselves. The decorations were warm and lush, and even the scent in the room had been thought out carefully. Something like cinnamon and apples.

Prescott had managed to make a place of unparalleled luxury, a place where you wanted to stay forever. That was quite an achievement.

"Thanks, James," she said, knowing better than to tip him. He'd be there when she checked out, and he knew that she'd make it worth his while to be at her beck and call while she was here.

"If you need anything," he said, making the word anything as long as possible, "call me. Star 77 on the telephone."

"I'll do that," she said, and he slipped silently out and closed the door after him.

She turned to the windows, looking out at the view of the ski lifts, their lights glowing in the dusk of coming evening. Her main goal here was to figure out how Prescott made this place so popular that people would pay just about anything to be here and be willing to go on an extensive waiting list for the privilege. It wasn't just the luxury—that could be bought. It was an intangible something—the skiing? atmosphere?—that people believed they'd get here and nowhere else.

She turned and went into the bathroom to shower and change so she could go back downstairs and start looking around. Have a meal at one of the restaurants. Maybe arrange for a massage. Begin her work. She sighed as she reached into the shower stall to turn on the water.

New Year's Eve

JACK RODE DOWN in the elevator that serviced his private quarters on the third floor of the main building, and stepped out into a side hallway in the south wing. He wore an off-white turtleneck sweater and dark slacks, his usual casual clothes. He never dressed up for New Year's and made sure that guests didn't feel they had to, either. Though some did. Tuxedos were brought out, and some shimmering dresses were worn, but most guests stuck to casual clothes like his.

He paused in the hallway, tugged at the cuffs of his sweater, then ran a hand over his longish, dark brown hair and got ready to "do" New Year's Eve at The Inn. He almost smiled. He felt as if he were going to the gallows, not a party.

The smile died. He'd be glad to get out of here soon. He found himself waking every morning wishing that was the day he could leave, that he could drive out of the gates and be off to discover what his life was all about.

"Boss, boss," someone called from the side exit. It was Malone, his personal assistant. The big man was in outerwear—a heavy black jacket, dark pants tucked into calf-high boots, and his lined face was flushed from the cold. He skimmed a watch cap off his short gray hair as he walked over to Jack. "Good, I caught you." He sounded a bit breathless.

The big man was usually the portrait of calm and control, and if he was rushing, there had to be trouble. "What's going on?" Jack asked.

"Drunks out by lift seven. One of them passed out." He lowered his voice to a rough whisper before he uttered the names of the offenders. Jack relaxed a bit. They were a couple, regulars at The Inn, and they had done this before. They expected to be able to get drunk and do what they wanted, and then expected it all to be kept private. Protect a guest's privacy at all costs was a mantra at The Inn.

"Where are they?" he asked.

"I got them back to their suite. He's in bed, but I didn't undress him." He shrugged and his voice lowered again. "Actually, he was half-undressed when I found him. She was saying something about skiing nude at midnight to celebrate." Malone shook his head. "She was down to her underwear when he passed out and Jerry called me. They could have frozen to death out there."

Nude skiing? It had been tried before. The same old same old. "Any signs of impaired breathing?" Jack asked.

"Naw, the guy's snoring. The woman ended up on the couch. She's feeling no pain."

"Drugs?"

"Not that I saw anywhere. I think it's just plain old booze that did them in."

He knew the couple had drinking problems, but he wasn't taking any chances. "Make sure someone checks on them every hour on the hour. Otherwise, let them be. They'll sleep it off. Waking with hangovers will be penalty enough for them."

Malone had been working for Jack only two months, but in that time, Jack had come to trust him completely. When Jack left Silver Creek, Malone had agreed to say right here and be part of the group that would keep things going. "I'll get Hector to do an hourly check until he's certain they're okay."

"Perfect." Jack glanced at his watch. "After you talk to Hector, you're off duty. Have some fun." He motioned behind him in the general direction of the heart of the lodge, the huge lounge area that had been cleared for the gala party. The fireplace would blaze, a band would play and the champagne would flow. Balloons and confetti were trapped in nets far above the planked floor, and at midnight the nets would open and the shimmering decorations would float down on the celebrants. The Inn did it every year, and every year the guests loved it.

Malone shook his head. "Thanks, but I think I'll pass. I'll hit the hay after I set things up with Hector."

As Malone headed back to the side exit, Jack turned and went in the opposite direction. He approached the huge rock arch that gave entry to the party, and he stopped, taking a look inside at the festivities, which were gaining momentum. The band was great, and the guests were already in the swing of things. Couples danced, while some mingled and drank champagne. Yet right then, it looked garish and forced to Jack.

"Cynic," he muttered, but didn't force himself to go inside. He decided right then and there he wasn't going to be part of the party. He'd go to his suite, do some of the paperwork he needed to have out of the way, then... What? Stare out at the night. Try to contact his close friends? Or just go to bed? He'd figure that out as he went along, but for now, he wasn't going into that party room.

He turned and ran directly into someone hurrying toward the party. There was a blur of contact, body hitting body, hands pressed to his chest, perfume in the air and a soft release of breath. The next instant he was staring down into the bluest eyes he'd ever seen. The color of true sapphires and framed with long, lush lashes.

"Oh, my goodness, good grief," a husky voice gasped. "I am so very sorry. I was hurrying and I thought you were going in, and I didn't think you were going to turn when you did."

As the woman spoke, she pushed back and gradually the full picture came into focus for Jack. He expected attractive, and he expected sexy, especially after that voice. But nothing he expected came up to the reality. The woman in front of him was stunning. She was probably half a foot shorter than he was, even with the high-heeled sandals she was wearing. Her reddish-blond hair was swept back and retained by diamond clips, but a few curls had escaped to frame her heart-shaped face and show off those remarkable eyes. A few freckles she'd made no attempt to hide with makeup dusted her short, straight nose. Full lips were a pale pink.

Then there was her body. A black silk blouse was cut low, exposing the soft fullness of high breasts, and gray clinging pants showed the flare of her hips.

He had to blink to focus on the moment, instead of the sight of her. She was talking and he caught up with her at "…hurt. I hope you aren't." She really did look concerned.

He made a guess at what she was asking so he could respond. "No damage done," he murmured. He usually made it his mission to meet every guest who stayed here, even if it was just to put a face to the name in the register. But he hadn't seen this face before. He would have remembered. "I'll survive. I'm just sorry I got in your way."

That brought a smile to her face, a flash of humor that did the strangest thing to him. It tightened his chest, and for a moment, he had to remind himself to breathe. He'd never had any rules about guests and getting involved with them. He went with the flow, and a few times, things had turned out just fine. He had an idea that something with her would be a bit better than just fine.

"I hit you, you didn't hit me," she said, her voice slightly breathless as she held out her hand to him. "I'm Jillian."

He took her hand in his, feeling the warmth and the delicateness of slender fingers. "I'm Jack Prescott," he responded.

One finely arched brow rose. "*The* Jack Prescott?"

He found himself smiling at that. "The one and only, at least around these parts."

A hand touched his shoulder, and as he reluctantly turned to find Malone there, he saw Jillian nod to him, then move away.

He wanted to tell her to stay, that this wouldn't take long, but he didn't get a chance. She quickly disappeared into the party. When he turned back to Malone and snapped, "What is it?" he knew he wouldn't be going upstairs anytime soon. The party looked awfully good to him now.

Chapter Two

Jack saw Malone stiffen at the tone in his voice and immediately regretted his display of annoyance. "I'm sorry. What's going on?"

The big man shrugged off the apology, obviously not expecting it or needing it. He moved closer and kept his voice low. "I called the doctor and he's on his way. Hector thought the guest was…" He shrugged. "His breathing bothered him, so I thought it was a prudent action."

"Good call. Keep me up to speed on it."

"You got it," Malone said.

"I'll be mingling with the guests at the party if you need me," he said, then added, "Do me a favor? There was a woman here when you came up…"

Malone nodded, his expression impassive. "I noticed."

"She said her name's Jillian. She's either a guest, or the guest of a guest. I'd like to know a bit about her."

Without a word, Malone took out a cell phone linked to the house line. He pressed three digits and said, "Give me a minute." Then he spoke into the phone. "Do we have a guest with the first name Jillian?"

He waited, listened, then flipped the phone shut. "Jillian O'Shay, checked in yesterday, asked for complete privacy. She's NW-330. She checked in alone."

He knew the suite and knew it was one of the priciest in the resort. It was usually booked months in advance, or on an annual reservation. "She's been here before?" he asked.

"No, first time, but she took over a reservation that was let go. Hayward Wills had it, and his assistant called to cancel for New Year's. He's supposedly in Paris."

Hayward Wills was a regular, a Hollywood actor who didn't mind who knew he was at The Inn. He'd caused problems before—mostly thanks to paparazzi—when he let it slip that he'd be at The Inn. One Thanksgiving, Wills had actually let some reporters in for a photo op and caused all sorts of problems. Jack wasn't sorry he'd canceled, and especially not when Jillian had been able to get his suite. "She had a standing request in for it?"

Malone shrugged. "I don't know, but I can find out, if you want."

"When you get a chance," Jack said, and celebration noises coming from the party seemed to swell. He glanced at his watch. Fifteen minutes to midnight. He told Malone to go and check with the doctor, then he turned and headed into the party.

He stepped into the lounge and scanned the room for

Jillian. He was ready to think she'd gone right through and into the north wing when he saw her. She was across the space, near the back, by herself. She wasn't speaking to anyone, but moving slowly toward the archway that led to the viewing area for the lifts. Then she stepped through and was gone.

He didn't bother to dissect what he was doing or why he was doing it, he just headed after her. He made his way through the throng of celebrants, smiling and nodding at their greetings, but his focus was on the archway across the room. He finally made it there, went through and saw her. She was in a side viewing area, the edges of which had been draped with glittering gold streamers. A champagne fountain sat near the entrance.

Only a handful of guests were in here, and none glanced at him in the doorway. Jillian was at the rear windows, her back to him, looking out at the ski lifts in the glow of security lights.

For a moment, as the music played behind him, he simply watched her watching the night. She was just as lovely as he'd thought the first moment he'd laid eyes on her, when he'd felt her hands on his chest and inhaled her delicate perfume.

Truth be told, the women who stayed at The Inn fell into one of two categories: those who felt they owned the world by virtue of their money or their power or both, and those who were clinging and needy. This woman didn't look like either. She had a presence about her, and he liked that. He'd never believed that a person should be the "be-all and end-all" to anyone. He certainly never wanted to be.

He finally moved, stopped to fill two flutes at the fountain, then carried them over to where Jillian stood. When he got within a few feet of her, he stopped and studied her profile. The slightly upturned nose, the dark lashes and tiny diamond studs at her ears. He watched her take a breath, then release it, and even though he couldn't hear it over the music, he was sure she'd just sighed. She was bored? Malone had said she'd checked in alone. And from what he could see she was still alone. Then again, maybe she was waiting for someone to show up.

He took a step toward her and spoke. "Hello, again."

His voice didn't seem to startle her, and for a moment he thought she hadn't heard him. Then he realized she'd not only heard him, but while he'd been studying her, she'd been watching him in the reflection of the windows. If he'd ever been the type to get embarrassed, he might have been then. But instead, he enjoyed the knowing smile on her lips when their eyes met in the reflection off the glass. He smiled back as she turned to face him.

Those blue eyes were touched with the sparkle of humor, and he couldn't remember the last time a woman's smile had affected him so much. He'd even forgotten he was holding the champagne until she glanced at the drinks. "You're really going to celebrate, aren't you," she said, her voice barely audible over the celebration behind them.

He moved closer, and his nostrils caught a hint of

roses that had nothing to do with the room. He recognized the scent as the one he'd inhaled when Jillian had run into him. Roses. Not the usual designer fragrances guests used. He lifted one of the glasses toward her. "Would you like to help me with one of these?"

She inclined her head slightly, then reached to take the narrow goblet. He felt her fingers brush his, then the goblet was in her hand and she was studying the fine crystal with the bubbly liquid. She took a sip, then lowered the glass, touched her tongue to her lips, and the smile returned. "Very, very nice."

It was then that he saw the glint of gold on her finger, a simple wedding band, but worn on the wrong finger. It was on her ring finger, but on her right hand. Married? Divorced? Widowed? Or maybe that was the latest fad, to wear a gold band wherever you wanted to wear it. Goodness knew, he'd seen enough gold rings in noses and ears and other bodily parts in the recent past. "Californian, private reserve," he said, and took a sip.

That smile flirted with her lips and eyes. Damn it, she was gorgeous—and intriguing.

She turned slightly to her right to put the flute on the window ledge, then cast him a quick glance from under dark lashes. "You're an impressive skier," she said.

He blinked at that. She'd seen him skiing? No, he didn't use the runs at the resort. He had his own place for skiing. "Who told you that?"

"I could say it's because this is all yours, but the truth is, I saw you skiing this morning."

He'd been off the property, up at "The Killer," a run he and his friends had used when they were teenagers. It was on the land he'd just purchased with the idea of expanding the runs at The Inn. Now, he wasn't sure what he'd do with the run, but he did know that no one was up there this morning. He'd been totally alone. He'd gone to ski it one last time before he left. "How could you do that?"

She leaned back against the window ledge, one leg crossing over the other, but her eyes never left his face. The smile didn't leave her lips, either. "I knew you didn't see me."

She was flirting and he knew it. But the idea of her watching him and his never knowing until now left him feeling unsettled. He wasn't sure why. It wasn't as if she were stalking him. "How did you even know it was me?"

"I didn't at first. I was out walking and got to this fence way up near the top, and this skier cut out of the trees. You were going so fast, you were a blur, cutting sideways, off to the south. You were gone almost before I saw you."

Guests didn't venture past the top area of the last lift. At least, he'd never seen one up there. "You were just out walking and you saw this skier rushing by, and you knew it was me?"

She smoothed her slacks with her right hand, a light flicking action that made the ring catch the lights in the room. "I could say that I saw you earlier and knew it was you, maybe even that I followed you up there. But I didn't. I was up there, saw you and a man who was fixing the stone wall. When I said to the man that I didn't know there was skiing up there, he said, 'That's Mr. Prescott and he owns the whole damn mountain.' Then he smiled and said, 'He can ski anywhere he wants to ski.'" Her eyes sparkled with humor. "Do you really own the whole damn mountain?"

"For now," Jack said. "And any time you want to ski the high slope, let me know. I'll be glad to take you up there."

She chuckled softly. "Me? I appreciate your offer, but I don't ski. I walk and climb, in boots. No skis."

"But you're at a ski resort."

She didn't answer as she reached for her drink again. He watched her tip the crystal up, finishing half the champagne, then reached to hand it to a server who had come to check on them. Finally she met his gaze. "I didn't come here for the skiing."

The celebration was building behind them, and the lights were changing, going from the twinkling glow to a series of dancing prisms that seemed to be everywhere. "Five minutes," someone called out, and there were cheers and clapping. Jack never looked away from Jillian. "Why *did* you come?"

"I have my reasons," she murmured.

He moved closer, so close he could see a pulse beating in the hollow at the base of her throat. "Let's forget about why you're here, and let's concentrate on celebrating the New Year."

She stared at him for a long moment. "Deal," she said.

The server was there and Jack handed him his empty goblet, then took the two gold noisemakers the man offered. Jack held one out to her. "Good old-fashioned noisemakers," he said as she took the foil trumpet from him and studied it. "Just pucker and blow."

"Sounds easy enough," she said.

At the same moment, the throng behind him started to count down. "Ten…nine…" He kept his eyes on Jillian. "Five…four…three…two…" Cheers, noise-makers, shouts and the strains of "Auld Lang Syne" filled the air. Confetti and balloons dropped from the ceiling and a clock chime sounded.

Jack looked at Jillian a foot from him, at the silver and gold confetti drifting down onto her hair and shoul-ders, setting the world aglitter. The magic hour. Midnight. The start of a new year. And he didn't stop to think of much other than the fact that her lips looked downright enticing at that moment. He dropped his noisemaker and reached over to touch her shoulders. He felt her slight startle of surprise at his touch.

"Happy New Year," he breathed, and as her eyes widened, he pulled her close and dipped his head toward her.

Everything was sensation—the sounds all around them, the scent of roses, the softness of her parted lips, the brush of her breasts against his chest, then her breath mingling with his. He kissed her, and the noises around them faded. The world centered on their connection, and Jack fell into a place he realized he liked very much.

Then, whatever was happening stopped. Jillian was moving back, her hands pushing gently on his chest again, just the way they'd been the first moment they met. He was looking into her blue eyes, and before he could do anything else, someone was slapping him on the back. A male voice, slurring from too much alcohol, shouted over the noises around them, "Happy New Year!" But Jack didn't turn to the speaker. He never looked away from Jillian.

He didn't miss the way she pressed her lips together any more than he missed the way she moved back to the windows. She smiled suddenly, but it was a different smile. If he didn't know better, he'd think she was embarrassed, but women like Jillian didn't get embarrassed by a simple kiss. They simply went with the flow, or they stopped it. Jillian had stopped it.

"Happy New Year," she murmured, then moved around him to leave.

He turned as she went out of the side area and into the main room. When he got to the stone archway, she was nowhere to be seen. Malone had said she was in the north wing, third floor, so he guessed that she'd headed back to her suite. A kiss was just a kiss for him—except for this kiss. He'd felt the impact of the connection on such a profound level that it still lingered.

A guest approached him, a rock star who was a regular when he wanted to dry out. Right now, however the pierced and tattooed man had a glass in his hand, and a goofy smile on his face. "Happy New Year, man," he mumbled thickly, then ambled off.

Jack caught the attention of one of his "overseers," people who discreetly kept an eye on guests with "problems." It was up to the overseer to curb any negative actions before they got out of control. He nodded toward the rock star and the man inclined his head in understanding, then casually wandered over to where the famous guest was refilling his glass at one of four bars in the room and starting to have a very hard time staying on his feet.

Jack glanced around, and knew it was time to leave. He certainly wasn't going to track Jillian down. And for the first time since he opened The Inn, he wasn't going to celebrate New Year's until the sun came up. Instead, he did what he'd decided to do before he ran into Jillian O'Shay. First he'd find Malone and check on the would-be nude skiers, then he'd go upstairs and either work or sleep or drink. Alone.

JILL MOVED AS SLOWLY as she could, although she wanted to run, and run fast. She'd let him kiss her. Damn it, she should have seen that coming. She wasn't stupid. She could tell when a man was attracted her, and she should have known how men like Jack Prescott looked at the world. Live for the day. If it feels good, do it. She'd been around enough of the privileged rich to know that most of them did what they wanted to do. Period.

She went out of the side room, but instead of going into the main room where the party was in full gear, she took the passageway to the elevator so she could go up to her suite. She heard someone behind her, and for a moment, she thought that Jack Prescott might have followed her. But when she stepped into the car and pressed the button for the third level, she saw the big man Jack had been speaking to earlier. He had his hand out to stop the door before it slid shut.

"Miss O'Shay?"

She stood very still, wondering what this guy did. Was he a goon who did Jack's bidding? Maybe it was his job to bring back women who were stupid enough to kiss Jack Prescott, then run away. "What do you want?" she asked, allowing her tone to show a touch of annoyance.

He acted as if she hadn't spoken at all. "You dropped this." He held out a security key card with his free hand.

Her room card? She felt in the pocket of her slacks and it was empty. "Oh," she said, taking the card from him, relieved that this had nothing to do with Jack at all. "I didn't realize I'd dropped it."

"No problem. If it happens again, just use any of the house phones and the door will be opened for you."

"Good to know," she said, and made herself stand very still while she met his gaze with her best I'm-rich-and-you're-just-the-person-to-serve-me look. She knew if she *were* incredibly wealthy and here to relax or hide out or any number of other things, that she'd be aloof and annoyed by being stopped on her way to doing what she wanted to do.

She was just about to order him to let go of the elevator

door when Jack suddenly came up behind the big man. "Anything wrong here?" he asked as he met her gaze.

All she could think of was the kiss. Talk about *wrong*. It took all her willpower not to scrub her hand over her mouth at that moment. As an alternative, she held up her security card. "I dropped it and this gentleman found it for me."

Jack never looked at the other man. "Glad he could help."

"Yes," she said and glanced at the big man's hand still restraining the door before she flicked her gaze to the man's face.

He immediately let go his hold and the doors slid shut, blocking Jack from her sight. She didn't breathe easily again until she was in her suite and the door was closed behind her.

It had been luck that she'd literally run into Jack Prescott downstairs; she couldn't have planned it better if she'd tried. She'd missed him at the ski slope and had to settle for the maintenance man telling her he owned the whole damn mountain. She'd wanted to meet him, wanted the opportunity to talk to him. She'd gone down to the party only because she'd been told that he was always at the big party and always had a great time. She'd wanted to find him, to make contact and see what sort of man he was.

She'd found him, all right, and she'd made contact with him. First, running into him, then she'd let him "find" her in the side room. Then the next contact. The kiss. She'd thought she'd be facing some sort of playboy, someone who partied hardy and whom she'd be able to meet and control that meeting.

Instead, she'd faced a man who hadn't seemed at all interested in the celebration, who obviously wasn't drunk or high, and who had taken control from the first. He'd been interested in her and he hadn't bothered to hide it. She'd tried to control the flirting, to keep her distance, but that hadn't worked. Not when midnight came and she found herself being well and properly kissed by the man. All of her well-thought-out plans could have been blown to bits—but she wouldn't let that happen. "Stupid me," she muttered.

She hadn't come to The Inn for any of that. She was here for one reason—to do a job. Now she gave in to the impulse to scrub the back of her hand across her mouth, then got her computer and laid it on a desk in the sitting area. She logged on and started to put in a summary of the day. She put in every observation she'd made about the workings of The Inn. She ended with *Met Prescott and will talk to him again.*

When she finished the report, she was taken aback to see it was almost two in the morning. She stretched to relieve the tension in her neck and shoulders, then moved to the windows that overlooked the ski runs. Snow was falling, playing through the glow of the lights that outlined the lifts. Far below, she could see a few people out in the snow, and she almost thought she could hear their laughter ringing in the air.

As she watched one couple, the man pulled the woman into his arms and kissed her for so long Jillian began to wonder if either one would pass out from not being able to breathe. Finally she turned away from the sight. She'd met Jack Prescott and she was ready to do what needed to be done. The next time they came face-to-face, she'd be the one to control the encounter. She'd be the one to get what she needed. She'd be the one to make sure she didn't do anything stupid again.

Although Jillian had been up since five that morning, she barely slept. The bed was wonderfully luxurious, the sheets felt like silk, but she did little more than doze off. Dawn broke, and as the light started to sneak into her room, she gave up trying to do any more sleeping. She got up, showered and dressed in designer jeans, a hand-knit blue pullover and leather boots that were supposed to be waterproof. Then she shrugged into a bright blue down jacket.

She took the time to glance out the window again. The runs were empty, but the lifts were kept running with their seats swinging eerily in the gray morning light. Obviously, most of the guests would be sleeping in after the celebration; she could take the opportunity to wander about the resort without a lot of people around her. She knew from past jobs that in a place like this, the staff didn't question a guest, no matter what they were doing or where they went. The staff was there to make sure the guest had a good time. She'd take advantage of that.

The privileges of the rich, she thought as she grabbed her room card, pushed it deeply into the pocket of her jacket and put a knit cap in the other pocket. She left her suite, and within moments was on the lower level, passing the great room where very little evidence of the New Year's celebration remained. It was almost as if it had never happened. The staff was rearranging the chairs and tables, and not one of them glanced at her as she went through to the archway that led to the ski shops and the entrance to the lifts.

She walked faster, down a sloped passageway lined by display windows that showed every type of ski equipment and attire a skier could want. She stepped down into a space that held a coffee bar, another of the many fireplaces, seats for viewing the lifts and a large side area that was dedicated to holding the guests' ski equipment.

When a server approached her with a pot of coffee, she took a cup, refused the offer of a croissant and crossed to the exit. Before she got there, the door quietly slid back for her. Another worker outside the door smiled, wished her a cheery good morning and asked if she needed any assistance with equipment or using the lifts.

She shook her head, and stopped to inhale air so cold it felt as if it might burn her lungs. She pulled her soft wool hat over her hair, then tucked her chin into her coat collar and squinted into the glare off the snow. Sunglasses. Damn it, she should have thought to bring the pair she'd worn yesterday. She turned and the attendant was still there. When they made eye contact, he came right over to her. "May I be of assistance?"

"I forgot my sunglasses."

She was going to ask where she could buy a pair, but he didn't give her a chance. He hurried inside, was gone for only a minute, then returned with several pairs of sunglasses in his hand. He held them out for her to choose.

She picked out a pair that she had no doubt cost several hundred dollars, and she knew that they'd be added to the bill. Ray would probably call her on it. But she simply put them on and murmured, "They're fine."

He went back inside, and she turned to the left instead of going toward the lifts. She'd gone that way yesterday, and even if Jack was up and skiing the high run, there wouldn't be any chance to talk to him. So she went south, intending to take a look at some of the private cabins that dotted the grounds in that direction.

The backdrop of the mountains was awesome, and the new snow clung to everything. She got to the south side of the resort by following a series of walking paths that had already been cleared from the recent snowfall, and saw the cabins snuggling into the land. As she walked, nothing stirred, and the only sounds to be heard were the low humming and metal whirring noises coming from the empty lifts.

She passed each cabin, studying them as she went. They might be called cabins, but they were as large as most homes. Fashioned out of rough wood and heavy timbers, they fit the snowy surroundings perfectly.

Smoke puffed out of the stone chimneys and most of the windows were blocked by closed curtains.

When she realized she was in front of the last cabin, she stopped. From there on, the path changed from cobbled to paved and widened enough to allow two cars to pass each other easily. She took a few more steps and realized she was looking down the road at a huge garage. A snowplow sat to one side, still and silent.

She decided to head back. She'd look down here later when she had her camera phone with her. As she turned, she found herself looking at a bright red Porsche and she knew it was the same one that had passed her the day she arrived here. It was parked at the bottom of stone steps that led up to the expansive porch area for the last cabin.

She was a bit surprised to see that the car had Nevada plates. They were also personalized, a phonetic take on the word revving—RVVVVVV. "Cute," she muttered sarcastically as she remembered the way the car had flown past her.

Before she could turn to go back, the cabin door opened and Jack Prescott stepped out onto the porch. He closed the door, did up the zipper on his leather bomber jacket, then looked up. Their eyes met and she realized that he hadn't stopped at just kissing her at midnight. He'd found another guest who had been more than willing to ring in the New Year with him.

She wasn't sure why that tasted so bitter in her mouth.

Chapter Three

Jack had thought about Jillian while he sat at the window in his suite sipping brandy and staring out at the night. He'd thought about a lot of things—about his leaving, about his life and about kissing Jillian at midnight. Now she was there, in the morning light, looking up at him, sunglasses hiding her eyes and white knit cap pulled low so just wisps of her hair were exposed.

He went down the steps and approached her. His smile was a product of his pleasure at seeing her again. "Good morning," he said.

She wasn't smiling, and his own expression shifted a bit. With her sunglasses in place, he couldn't see the expression in her eyes, and he wished he could. "Good morning," she responded, and her breath curled into the cold air.

"What are you doing out and about this early?"

"I couldn't sleep," she said.

"I can relate to that," he admitted.

"Yeah," she said as she pushed her hands into the

pockets of her jacket. She glanced away from him to look at the other cabins. "You've got quite a setup here. Gorgeous country. Nice layout. Privacy. Everything a guest could ask for."

"I'd be glad to show you around," he heard himself say.

"Excuse me?" she asked, looking back at him.

He didn't think he'd ever met a woman like her. No makeup and harsh morning light. Yet she looked beautiful. He put his hands in the pockets of his leather jacket to keep from touching her. "We could start with me showing you what a great breakfast you can get at The Inn."

She hesitated, then glanced at the cabin. "Aren't you busy?"

He knew what she thought and barely restrained a burst of laughter. She thought he'd been in the cabin having some sort of sexy romp with a rich snow bunny and now he was hungry. He'd make sure he disabused her of that notion over breakfast. "No, I'm not," he said.

She arched an eyebrow. "Are you sure?"

He wouldn't wait until breakfast. "Listen, I was just here to do a favor for a friend."

"Oh," she said softly, the single word speaking volumes.

He exhaled roughly. "Let me explain. I—"

She shook her head. "That's okay."

He wasn't used to having to beg a woman to have breakfast with him, or to feeling that he had to explain his sex life to her. He decided to ask one last time, then let it go. "Breakfast?"

Unexpectedly, she agreed. "Sure, breakfast. I'm starving."

"Let's go," he said, and started toward his Porsche. He'd parked it at the cabin when he'd come back from an attorney meeting two days ago, when he'd been hurrying back to see Cain Stone, one of his closest friends, before he left the cabin to go back to Las Vegas, where he lived. Cain had found a life for himself, a very different life from what he'd lived for thirty-eight years. He'd been a hotel/casino owner, and although he was still that, he was now a family man, with a new wife and stepdaughter. The change was dramatic, and one of the reasons Jack had started to look at his own life more closely.

"Let me get the heater going and we'll—"

She stopped him just as he grabbed the door hasp. "No, I'd rather walk."

By the time he said, "Sure, no problem," she'd turned and was starting back down the path toward the main lodge. He fell in beside her, matching his stride to hers, and felt the brush of her jacket sleeve against his. It was a random contact, something that happened all the time when two people walked together, but it had the effect of making him all the more aware of the woman at his side.

"So, is that red bomb yours or your friend's?" she asked out of the blue.

He cast a sideways glance at her, but she was looking straight ahead, her chin lifted and the growing wind teasing the tendrils of hair that had escaped from her cap. "You mean the car? It's mine. Why?"

"I was driving the car you left in your dust on the highway a few days ago." She flashed a quick glance in his direction. "The car you almost sideswiped when you passed me."

He knew exactly what she was talking about, and it made him start to smile. "Oh, you were driving that SUV that was stopping in the middle of the road for no apparent reason?"

"It was slippery and I was being cautious," she countered.

"Oh," he murmured, mimicking the way she'd said that very word when he'd told her why he'd been at the guest unit.

She ducked her head. "You almost cut me off."

"I gave you plenty of room," he countered.

"Inches, mere inches," she insisted.

He touched her arm, stopping her in the middle of the path, and she looked up at him. The glasses reflected back his own image instead of letting him look into her eyes. He really hated those mirrored glasses, he thought as he held up his hands a good three feet apart to make his point. "Feet, many feet."

He'd hoped to make her smile, and he did. In the dull light of morning, the expression seemed to light up everything in its path. No wonder he'd kissed her last night!

"Let's get real," she murmured, and she reached for his hands, pressing her palms to the backs of his hands. The contact was surprisingly warm as she pushed a bit and brought his palms within an inch of each other.

"Inches," she murmured. "Inches." Then she drew back and strode off toward the entrance by the lifts.

He caught up with her before she got to the automatic doors. "Is it Jillian or Jill?" he asked.

She looked up at him, the glasses reflecting back his image. "Whichever you prefer."

He didn't have to think twice. "Jillian it is. I'm not big on nicknames."

"Jack is your full name?"

"Jack Elliot Prescott."

"What number?"

"What?"

"As in, the first, the second, the fifteenth? Like the King Henrys in England?"

"First, last and only. Did you think I'd have a lineage?"

She shrugged. "I didn't know. I just knew you owned this place and the whole damn mountain. A few people said that you own most of the town, too."

He didn't know if he liked the fact she'd been talking about him to people around here. Then again, he knew he was the subject of gossip more often than not. "Hearing the truth depends on who you talk to."

"Now, that's deep," she said. "And I can't get too philosophical until I have some food." She grimaced expressively. "Actually, I can't do much thinking in this cold. I'm not used to it." She turned to go to the doors.

A wind was building and it pushed the cold, making it more raw and cutting. He followed her, and when the barriers opened, they both went inside.

"What are you used to?" he asked as she stopped and tugged off her hat.

"California weather." She pushed the hat into her pocket, then took off the glasses.

Eyes as blue as the sky were turned to him now. God, she really was lovely, down to and including the way wispy curls of her hair brushed her cold-flushed skin.

"Snow isn't something you get there unless you head up to the mountains," she said.

"I've heard that Californians have trouble with any weather other than warm and sunny."

Humor flashed in her eyes. "Rain tends to cause havoc."

And Jillian O'Shay was causing havoc in him, he thought. "I bet it does," he said, and as she walked farther inside, he matched her stride. When she hesitated at the arched stone opening at the main room, he motioned to their left. "This way," he said, and they went together into the middle corridor that ran deeply into the north wing. They passed the alcove they'd been in the night before, and she didn't spare it a glance.

The Eagle's Nest, the main restaurant in the lodge, was just past the bar and a lounging area. As they approached the entry to the restaurant, one of his staff, a tall, thin kid with white teeth that seemed to glow against his deep tan, approached them. "Good morning, sir."

"Morning, Shane," Jack said. "Breakfast for two."

"Yes, sir." Shane led the way through the stone arch and down into the main dining area.

Jack took the step down into the central area of the

restaurant and didn't realize that Jillian had stopped dead in her tracks until he almost walked into her. "What's wrong?" he asked, thinking the view through the bank of windows across the room might have caught her attention. Even after seeing the same view every day for most of his life, it still had the power to make him stop and look. But when she spoke, he knew it wasn't the view.

"There's no one in here," she said as she turned to face him.

He knew there wouldn't be anyone this early on New Year's Day. He'd liked the idea of being alone with Jillian for a meal, but *she* didn't sound pleased. "No noisy guests," he said.

His confusion grew when she said, "You know, you must have a ton of things to do."

"No, I don't." It was a lie, but he didn't care. "I need breakfast and you said you were starving, so let's eat."

He'd known her for such a short time, but when she continued to stand where she was and glanced up to her left, he realized that was her action when she was weighing her options. For the life of him, he didn't know why. It was a simple choice—eat or starve. Although maybe for her, the choice was eat with him or come back later and eat by herself.

He didn't have to have a brick drop on his head to know when a woman wasn't interested in being with him. But with Jillian, he was getting mixed signals.

Then he wondered if her problem was seeing him

come out of the cabin and thinking he'd been there with a woman. He hadn't been, but even if he had, he didn't expect her to worry about that. They barely knew each other, and if she were jealous…? No. That was ridiculous. Stupid. They'd kissed at midnight. He'd done that more often than he could remember. It was tradition. It was done.

"So how about it?" he asked, refusing to speculate on why he was really hoping she'd stay and have breakfast with him.

Suddenly she nodded. "Sure, why not?"

Why not, indeed? he thought, but all he said was, "Shane, give us a table with a great view."

Shane had hung back until then, but now he smiled at them. "Sir, every table in the Eagle's Nest has a great view."

He liked this kid. "Then pick one for us," Jack said, and Shane led them to a table in the center of the window area. If there had been other diners, it would have had little or no privacy.

Shane helped Jillian slip off her jacket and hang it on one of the custom hooks inset on the back of her high wooden chair. Jack did the same, then took the chair opposite Jillian. "I think we're the only ones who didn't overdo the celebration last night," he said.

She shrugged at that as she ran a finger over the silver charger that was part of the table setting. "I guess being the owner of this place has its drawbacks."

She has no idea, he thought. "It can, but I've never

been one to get soused at New Year's." He altered that statement. "At least, not in recent years."

"So, there was a time when you partied?"

He leaned forward, resting his forearms on the table. "I had my moments. How about you?"

"Hasn't everyone?" she countered, and the topic was over when she swept her gaze around the empty restaurant. "You have quite a resort here," she said. "Not too rustic, not too formal. Not too open, not too closed. High-end, but not in your face."

That took him aback. Guests weren't usually sitting around critiquing his business. They just enjoyed it. They used what was here and didn't notice much of anything around them, unless they were disappointed or demanding more than they were given. "Is that good or bad?"

Her blue eyes met his. "Obviously very good."

"Or you wouldn't be here?"

She blinked at that. "Of course."

A waiter, Ellis, set down a tray with several silver pots and two heavy mugs. The dark-haired man poured a cup from one pot in front of Jack. "Your breakfast roast, sir," he murmured, then glanced at Jillian while his hand hovered over the selection of pots. "I brought some cinnamon roast, continental roast, hazelnut and a mild decaffeinated blend."

Jack watched Jillian shake her head and say, "No coffee. Green tea, naturally decaffeinated, with clover honey and lemon."

"Right away," Ellis said, and took the tray with him when he left.

She sat back a bit in the chair, resting both hands palm down on either side of the charger. He liked that her nails had only a clear polish on them, and they weren't unnaturally long, but neat ovals. And that wedding band on the right hand. He would have liked to ask about it, but he let that go. Later, he'd find out.

"So, you were doing a favor for a friend," she said out of the blue. "Do you call all your guests friends?"

It took him a second to figure out what she was talking about. "No, not at all." And he saw his opening for an explanation about his presence at the cabin. He wasn't going to let her interrupt this time. "I was in the cabin by myself, picking up a watch for Cain Stone. He's one of my closest friends. We grew up together. He was here over the Christmas holidays, and he left in a rush. He was distracted by…" No. No need to explain about Cain and Holly right now. "He had something come up and he had to get back to Las Vegas. He couldn't take everything with him, but he didn't mean to leave his watch behind. It was on the table by the bed." He fished in his pocket and took out a plain silver expansion-band wristwatch. He looked down at it. "It's nothing special, as far as its cost goes, but it's important to him."

"Cain Stone." She said the name softly as Jack put the watch back into his pocket. "He owns the Dream Catcher Casino and Hotel in Las Vegas, doesn't he?"

"Yes, as a matter of fact, he does."

"Does he have investments around here?"

That question struck him as odd, as did her earlier comments about the restaurant. He sat back in his chair and took time to sip some coffee before he answered her. "He's from Silver Creek and the town's been growing by leaps and bounds." He knew he hadn't answered her at all, but she didn't call him on it.

He had a question for her. "So are you going to tell me why you came to The Inn?"

She shrugged and glanced to her left out the windows. "I didn't have anything to do over the holidays, and The Inn is *the* place to be, or so I was told." She glanced back at him. "Do you have any competition?"

"Not really."

"What if you did?"

"It wouldn't matter. If people want to be here, they'll be here. If they don't, so be it."

"And if your rooms were empty, then what?"

The waiter was back with a silver pot of tea and crystal dishes, one with honey in it with a twisting spoon to serve it, and another with a carefully dissected lemon. He laid it out in front of Jillian, then stood back. "Sir, does your regular order stand?"

"Yes, that'll be fine," Jack said.

The waiter took Jillian's order for a mushroom omelet—shiitake, steamed, not grilled—and seven-grain toast. Then Jack watched Jillian pour tea into her cup, carefully spoon in some honey, then dip a wedge of lemon in. She swirled the fruit around in the steaming liquid, then took it out and laid it neatly on the side saucer. She cradled her mug, lifted it and looked at him over the top before she took a sip. He must have been smiling, because she frowned slightly and asked, "What?"

"Unlike coffee, tea drinking seems to be a science."

She sipped some, then put the mug back down. "I don't know. There's cinnamon roast, continental roast, hazelnut and, what did he say, a mild decaffeinated blend? What happened to black or with cream and sugar?"

He chuckled. "Okay, you've got me. I have to admit that we probably have a hundred different blends and, on top of that, some guests bring their own or call ahead to special order what they want."

"And I bet you never miss a beat. A guest says, 'I want a Columbian bean, harvested in the spring on the west side of the mountain, ground on a Tuesday when it rained and blended with almond extract.' Sure, no problem."

He chuckled. "You're not far off the mark."

Jillian liked his laughter. Shoot, she liked a lot of things about this man. He was attractive, in an easy, sexy sort of way. He didn't appear to be the type who went in for razor cuts, or skin care, and even his clothes were ordinary—jeans and a pullover, no obvious designer labels. She glanced at the mug by him. "So, what's your poison?"

His smile changed to one with a touch of wryness. "Coffee. Plain old ground coffee. I'm not even sure what country the beans come from. All I ask is that it's hot, strong and not deprived of its caffeine." He motioned to her mug of tea. "I'm not sure I've actually seen anyone drink green tea before."

A waiter appeared, and with an apologetic murmur of "Please excuse me" to Jillian, he leaned down to whisper something to Jack. She stared down into her tea, but thought she heard something about a "huge problem in the kitchen." She looked up as Jack rose to his feet.

"I'm sorry. I've got to take care of something. I'll be right back." He went with the waiter out of her line of sight. She turned and saw the two men go through a door that was almost hidden in the side wall.

For a moment she caught a glimpse of everything white and stainless steel, then the door closed. She sat back and looked out the windows. So Jack hadn't been at the cabin with a woman. It shouldn't make any difference to her, but for some reason she felt a degree of relief. Stupid, she thought, and reached for her tea. She sipped more hot liquid and glanced around. She'd meant what she'd said about this place. It hit a perfect balance in every aspect of its management. Down to and including the owner being intimately involved in the day-to-day operations.

The food came moments later, at least hers did, and the waiter offered an explanation. "Mr. Prescott said to enjoy your meal, and he'll be back with you as soon as he can."

She stared at Jack's coffee mug across the table from her. She stared at it for a long moment, then glanced at her food. Perfectly cooked. Perfectly presented. But she didn't touch it. Instead, she made a split-second decision and got up. She left her jacket on the chair and headed across the room. She had an opportunity to see the kitchen without looking suspicious and she was going to take it. They'd just think she was looking for Jack.

She didn't hesitate to push open one door, and her impression of stainless steel and white had been correct. Stainless steel was everywhere, and where it wasn't, white tiles and enamel took over. She'd seen operational kitchens in a lot of hotels and resorts, but this one was most impressive, state of the art and laid out in a perfect flow pattern. She moved farther inside, getting furtive glances from the workers, but no one stopped her.

She stayed off to the side, away from the bank of stoves and grills under huge exhaust fans, moving past the prep area where four sous-chefs were busily chopping up fresh vegetables and fruit. One of them looked up, met her gaze and smiled before ducking his head to keep working. She heard a voice, then looked ahead near huge metal doors that she knew fronted a walk-in freezer. Jack appeared from a side area with a man in a dark navy coverall, wearing a heavy tool belt and carrying what looked like black hoses.

She was ready for the moment he saw here with "Oh, my goodness, what a fancy kitchen!" or "I was just looking for you." But now she realized how stupid that was. She'd been too impulsive coming in here, and she knew she could do more harm than good by being caught by Jack. She inched back, keeping her eye on

Jack talking to the repair guy, and finally reached the doors. She made sure he wasn't looking when she ducked out.

She hurried back to the table, sat down and picked up her fork. In less than a minute, Jack was back. She looked up as he sat down, and said, "Trouble?"

"Just a problem with refrigeration." He smiled after he said that. "Too bad we can't do what the pioneers around here used to do for refrigeration."

"Which was?"

"They buried their perishables in the snow and dug them out when they needed them. I suspect they found stuff at the spring thaw that they forgot they'd stored."

She smiled and speared a piece of mushroom. "Simple and to the point," she said, then popped the food into her mouth. It took all of her control not to spit it out. It was cold, and the butter used to sauté it had congealed. She gamely chewed and said, "This is really delicious."

The waiter slipped Jack's food onto the charger in front of him, and she realized that Jack Prescott, despite being surrounded by the unbelievable luxury he'd helped create, was a plain man. Plain coffee, plain clothes, plain food. His usual appeared to be two eggs over easy, cottage potatoes, bacon and whole-wheat toast. Plain and simple.

They ate in silence. She managed to get down a bit of her food and knew it would have been delicious hot, but it turned barely edible cold. She fiddled with what was left, then laid her fork down and finished her now tepid tea. She'd barely put her mug down before Jack spoke, and her stomach knotted.

"What were you doing in the kitchen?" he asked as casually as one would ask for someone to pass the salt.

"Excuse me?" she said, buying time.

"Glenn, the original chef, said he saw a beautiful woman in the kitchen. You're the only beautiful woman around." He smiled at her, and a dimple to the left of his lips showed up again.

"I...I was looking for you."

He inclined his head. "Really?"

"Yes, really. I hate eating alone." She picked up her napkin and laid it over the rest of her meal. "And you were gone for so long. I was...I guess I was curious."

Jack finished his coffee and almost before the mug hit the table, the waiter was there refilling it for him. "Curious, huh? You know what they say about curiosity...?"

She didn't want to think about dead cats. "Of course. My dad always said that I'm far too curious for my own good." That was the truth. She always wanted to know the why and what of any situation. That's probably why she did so well getting information for her bosses. Facts intrigued her. Digging to get those facts intrigued her even more.

Jack sat forward, resting his forearms on the tabletop. "Curiosity isn't all bad," he murmured.

Damn it. She felt heat rise in her cheeks and tried to distract herself by putting her silverware on the napkin covering her uneaten food. "It's gotten me into more than one mess," she admitted.

He studied her openly for a long moment, then asked, "What sort of messes?"

She sat back, needing a bit more space between them, and when she began to twist the plain gold band on her right hand, she made herself stop. Nerves were churning in her, but she didn't want him to know that. And it didn't help that she had the silly urge to tell him about when she was a child and got herself stuck in a clothes hamper just to see if she'd fit, or how she took apart her father's new clock radio to find out what made it light up at night. She settled for, "Childish things. You know."

He smiled wryly. "Yes, in fact, I do know about childish impulses and getting in trouble."

"Aha," she said. "Do tell me what a rich kid does to get into trouble around here."

He stared at her for what seemed like forever before he took a swallow of his coffee, then he sat back. "Were you ever curious about what would happen if you climbed into an empty wine barrel at the top of a ski run, then rolled down?"

She laughed at that, really laughed, and it felt good. The knot in her stomach loosened, and the tension building in her shoulders and neck eased. "You did that?"

He nodded. "Twice."

"Twice?"

"The first time Cain said I was using my hands, and

that's why the barrel went down straight. He dared me to do it again with no hands."

"And you did?"

"You bet I did, and I crashed halfway down, went sideways into a tree. The barrel was history, and I almost was, too."

Her smile slipped. "You were hurt?"

He hesitated, then turned to his right, put his hand by his ear and pushed back his hair. It exposed a pale, jagged scar that ran from behind his ear toward the back of his head, then up into his hair. She couldn't explain why the sight of the scar made the tension come back full force.

Then Jack was turning, looking at her, and he actually smiled. "I almost scalped myself, or at least that's what my dad said. All I could think of was going back with another barrel and proving it could be done."

Her eyes widened. "Did you?" she asked softly.

He nodded. "Of course."

"How many times did it take you to succeed?"

He leaned closer to her and said in a low voice, "Would you believe five?"

"You don't give up easily, do you?"

That was when he laid his hand over hers, pinning it to the tabletop. "I don't give up on anything...or anyone," he said softly.

Chapter Four

Jack felt Jillian start at his touch, but he didn't remove his hand. This woman intrigued him. He wasn't sure what to make of her, but he wanted to figure her out. No one else had asked him how many times he'd had to take the dreaded barrel run to prove to Cain he could do it. And although that was a small detail in the scheme of things, it got his attention.

Now she felt warm under his hand, and she didn't pull away. "What do you have planned for today?" he asked.

She shrugged, and now she withdrew her hand from under his. "I don't know, maybe relax and look around here. I haven't seen much of the resort."

Interesting, he thought. She sounded more like a tourist than someone who took this all for granted. "Sounds boring to me," he said. "How about seeing the town?"

She met his eyes. "Is Silver Creek large enough to fill up a few hours?"

"If you're into doing the antique store, boutique, tourist-trap thing. Not the real Silver Creek, of course."

She loosely laced her fingers together on the tabletop. The ring glinted in the light coming in the windows. "Is the real Silver Creek where you raced in wine barrels?"

"No, that spot of infamy isn't in town at all. It's north of here, higher up into the mountain."

"Do you return to the scene of the crime very much?"

He'd never even thought about the wine barrel incident or about going back to see where it had happened—until she asked him. "Not recently."

"Is there a monument there? You know, 'On this spot, on such and such a date, our very own Jack Prescott risked life and limb to prove he could navigate a hill in a wine barrel without using his hands.' Something like that?"

He chuckled. "Nothing like that. Just the offending tree."

She stood, reached for her jacket and slipped it on. "I think I'll just hang out here."

He didn't want her to "just hang out" by herself. He wanted to spend more time with her, so he made her an offer he hoped she couldn't refuse. "Do you want to see the scene of the crime?"

Her fingers on the zipper of her jacket stilled and her eyes met his. "The infamous wine-barrel-challenge location?"

He pushed back his chair and as he stood, he found himself so close to Jillian that he caught a hint of roses in the air. "Would you like to see it with me? It's maybe two miles or so by road from here. If you hike, it's a lot closer." He grabbed his jacket and put it on.

"You can leave here?" She made a vague sweep with her hand. "Won't last night's revelers wake up with raging hangovers and need a ton of service mixed with hand-holding?"

"They sure will, but that's what my staff is trained to do. Besides, I'm no hand-holder, no matter who it is."

The waiter had been standing just off to Jack's left, obviously waiting for a break in the conversation. When it came, he spoke up quickly. "Sir, Mr. Malone asked me to tell you that he needs to speak to you right away."

"Tell him I'm busy," Jack replied, but the waiter interrupted earnestly.

"He said it's very important. It needs your immediate attention."

So much for what he wanted to do. He looked at Jillian. "A rain check?" he asked.

"Sure."

"Maybe later today?"

She shook her head. "I think I'll go with my first plan and just hang out and relax."

"Okay. Enjoy yourself," he said.

"That's the plan," she said, then walked away.

He watched her leave, then turned to the waiter. "Where is he?"

"His office."

"Great," he muttered. He'd find Jillian later.

The day was eaten up with business, and Jack hated every minute of it. The first crisis was their liquor provider, whose warehouse staff had gone on strike and deliveries were not forthcoming. Then he'd had to take a phone conference from his lawyer and set up a power of attorney for while he was gone. Then a ski lift broke down. By evening, he was fed up. This place ate him up and spit him out. For all the money he had, and for all the control he thought he had, he was a slave to his possessions. It was that simple. Not an hour of the day went by that he didn't need to take care of something. God, he couldn't wait to leave. Three days and he was out of here. He didn't care where he went, but he was going.

Meanwhile, he didn't want to be alone. He put in a call to Jillian's room, but it went to her voice mail. He hung up, then called Gordie's cell phone. Ivan Gordon, the doctor at the clinic, was another member of his small circle of good friends. Cain and Josh, the son of the sheriff, had their own lives going on, but Gordie was like him. He, too, had a job that never let him relax, and he was alone in his personal life.

He found out Gordie was at The Inn, checking on the couple who had survived a nearly fatal bout of alcohol poisoning after trying to ski in the nude. He contacted him, and his friend was in Jack's suite fifteen minutes later. The two men faced each other across the large leather ottoman, where a tray with a bottle of brandy sat between them. As they sipped from their snifters, Gordie studied Jack from under lowered lids.

Gordie had been the nerd in town growing up, as nonathletic as they came, except for skiing, which he'd developed some competence at. But he'd grown into a man who was a fabulous doctor, who chose to practice in the town's clinic. He'd lost a lot of his hair and he wore glasses now, over brown eyes. His usual clothes, corduroys with sweaters and heavy boots, never changed. He settled lower in the couch.

"You're still going?" Gordie asked.

Jack nodded, sipped his brandy, then tried to explain what he was going to do and why. Gordie listened, nodded, sipped his drink and waited until Jack ran out of things to say. Then he simply said, "Go for it."

Gordie was the first person who hadn't challenged his decision. "Thanks," he said, touched by the simple support from his friend.

The doctor raised his glass. "Here's to finding what you're looking for."

"Yes," Jack said, lifting his own drink in a salute. "To what I'm looking for." He just hoped he'd know it when he found it.

JACK AWOKE WITH A START the next morning and sat up in bed. He'd had a dream. He wasn't sure what it was about exactly, but Jillian had been in it. There had been the wine barrel, snow, laughter, her giving him a medal. He snorted with laughter at the ridiculousness of the whole thing, and stopped when the simple act of laughing made him feel as if his head would fall off. He eased up to a more upright position and saw that it was barely seven.

Cautiously, he got to the side of the bed and paused before standing. He and Gordie had finished off all the brandy and had started on a bottle of scotch they'd found in the bar. They'd been there for hours, and had only stopped when Gordie had insisted he had to get back to the clinic. Jack had ordered a car and driver for the doctor and had a server help him out; the poor guy had barely been able to stand. Gordie had hugged Jack before he left, then said, "Never mix drinks."

"Yeah, never mix drinks," Jack muttered as he stood and steadied himself. When he felt reasonably certain he could make it to the bathroom, he padded naked in that direction.

Twenty minutes later, after a long shower and dressing in jeans, a chambray shirt and his favorite boots, he felt more human. When he stepped into the living area, he wasn't surprised to see Malone sitting on one of the couches with an open folder in his hands. The big man glanced up at Jack. "Morning, boss."

"Same to you." Jack crossed to the other couch, where he'd sat last night with Gordie, and sank into the soft leather. Now, instead of a tray of brandy sitting on the ottoman, there was a tray with a carafe of coffee and a bottle of aspirin sitting next to one of two mugs. Malone had obviously either brought it up or had it delivered. The man knew everything. Jack reached for the aspirins, popped two in his mouth, then downed them with coffee. "Thanks for that," he said to Malone as he sat back with the mug in his hand.

"No problem."

Malone was in gray today, a real lightening-up for

him. Black was his usual color of choice. "I was wondering if you'd seen—?" Jack began.

"Miss O'Shay?"

Damn it, the man *was* a mind reader. "You know where she is?"

"I'd guess she's in her room."

He said the right words, but there was something else there. "And?"

"Well, boss, I was just thinking that she doesn't seem to be like most of the guests you get here."

He knew what he meant. "No, she doesn't."

"I mean, she thanks people when they help her."

Jack would have laughed at that, but he knew he'd regret it. "Odd, huh?"

"And she has this tiny camera phone that she takes pictures with."

"Doubly odd to take pictures with a camera phone."

Malone wasn't put off by the sarcasm. "I found out she's from San Francisco and single. Can't find out where she gets her money, and she's not known on the usual club circuit."

"Wow, you nailed her. Polite, takes pictures and doesn't party," he muttered.

Malone let it go. "What's set for today?"

"Nothing, absolutely nothing. I gave my lawyer all the information for the power of attorney and he's dealing with the queries on the property. Nothing more for me to do today."

"So you're still leaving?"

"In a few days," Jack confirmed. "As soon as the paperwork's signed and the staff is in place."

The big man nodded, then stood up as he closed the file. "I've got things to do," he said over his shoulder on the way to the exit.

After Malone was gone, Jack said, "Yeah. Things to do, people to see…that's my life."

He reached for the phone, punched in the number for Jillian's suite and waited while it rang four times. Just when he thought it was going to go to the voice mail, she picked up. "Yes?" she answered in a sleep-softened voice.

He had an instant image of her, her hair tousled, her eyes heavy with sleep. "It's Jack."

There was silence, then a soft, "Good morning."

"I woke you."

"No…well, yes, but I need to get up."

"Are you interested in seeing the wine barrel tree?"

More silence before she said, "I'd like that, but I can't go until noon or so."

"Fine, no problem."

"Where should I meet you?"

He'd thought he'd go to her room, but if she wanted to meet him, he'd meet her. "There's a bar when you come off your elevator. It's to the left when you're on the way to the main room."

"Sure, I know it."

"Noon?"

"Noon," she said, and hung up.

AT TWO MINUTES to twelve, Jack headed down to the bar. He expected he'd have to wait, but he didn't. Jillian was at a small table near the entrance, and she spotted him immediately. She rose as he got close, and he could see she was wearing a silky white shirt with slim jeans and calf-high boots. Her hair was pulled up and off her face into a ponytail, and she smiled when she saw him.

He'd heard someone say that everyone should have one person who smiled when they saw them. For today, for him, Jillian was that person. "Are you ready to go?" he asked when he reached her.

"All set," she said, and plucked her jacket from a side chair and put it on.

He spoke to a server close to them. "Ian, have them get the car in number twelve and bring it around to the side door."

"Yes, sir." The man would have hurried off, but Jillian stopped him.

"No, wait," she said, and looked at Jack. "We'll take my car." She wasn't asking, she was telling.

"You don't like my red beast?"

"It's nice, but I don't think it's the right car for driving higher into the mountains." She held her hand up, palm toward him. "I know you've lived here all your life, and you know this place, but you can't tell me that your Porsche doesn't have its moments when the tires leave the road?"

No, he couldn't, and he wouldn't. "It does have its

moments," he agreed. "That's why he's getting my other car, a four-wheel-drive beast."

Faint color rose in her cheeks. That was another way Jillian O'Shay differed from the usual female guests at The Inn. She actually blushed. "Oh, I'm...I'm sorry."

"No problem," he said, and nodded to the server to get it.

The man hurried off, and Jack started in the same direction, with Jillian falling in step beside him. "Sorry, I should have known you'd have a sensible car for this weather."

He cast her a slanted look. "I have a car for every day of the week."

Jillian almost missed her step, but she recovered so quickly that she thought he hadn't noticed. At least she hoped he hadn't. "Really," she said, without meeting his gaze.

"No," she heard him murmur, and Jillian realized he was kidding. It was a joke. She kicked herself mentally, and tried to think of something to say. But she kept her mouth shut as they walked.

The man's worth had to be in the stratosphere. He had this resort, owned most of the town. Heck, he owned "the whole damn mountain." That was why she was here with him now. She really wanted to see another part of that mountain, not just the developed area. Ray had agreed with her when she'd called him yesterday. "Go and look and see what you think," he'd said. "We need input on the location and on what Prescott is thinking right now about the land. Get back to me."

She'd intended to call Jack when she awoke this morning, but hadn't had to. He'd called and made the offer without her having to say a thing. She'd insist that she drive her car, and she'd see the land. It had seemed simple. She'd even pushed her camera phone in her pocket to try to get some shots. Then things had started to shift. Maybe it had been at noon today when she'd first seen Jack, but whenever, she could honestly admit to herself that nothing would ever be simple with this man. Then he'd countered her idea of driving with his own idea. He'd made an offer she couldn't refuse.

By the time they got to the side entrance, the silence between them was unbroken. Jack nodded to a few guests, said a couple of murmured good-mornings. As they stopped by the closed door to the outside, Jack glanced to his left and called out, "Ivy?"

Jillian saw a tall, middle-aged woman coming out of a side door marked *Private*. She looked up and as soon as she spotted Jack, she was all smiles. As she approached, Jillian could see she was rather attractive, with gray-blue eyes and a slender build. She wore a navy pantsuit with a white shirt and a discreet brass name tag. *Ms. Dorsett, Housekeeping.* "Good afternoon, sir."

"Have you seen Malone anywhere?" Jack asked.

She frowned. "I believe the last time I saw him, he was on his way to one of the guest units, number ten. He said something about checking on a situation."

Jack frowned. "Anything serious?"

"I believe he was…" She darted a look at Jillian, then finished with, "Doing a follow-up with the problem of a Mr. Daniels."

"Leave a message for Malone with Lionel. Tell him to do what he thinks best and that I'm going to be off grounds for a while. He can brief me when I get back."

"Yes, sir," she said, then nodded to Jillian and headed off.

As Jack turned to the door, Jillian asked, "Guest problems?"

He didn't answer as he pushed open the door and let her precede him into the frigid morning air. Parked at the bottom of the steps was a large gray SUV with the motor idling. The minute they appeared, a man got out and hurried around, nodding a "Great day, sir," as he opened the passenger door for Jillian.

She had to use a side strap to pull herself up into the car and by the time she settled into the leather bucket seat, Jack was behind the wheel, doing up his seat belt. The attendant spoke across her to Jack as she did up her belt. "It's all gassed up and ready to go, sir."

Jack thanked him, and after the attendant closed the door, he made a U-turn and headed toward the gates.

Jillian waited until they were through the gates and turning north, away from the town, before she tried again. "I thought that confidentiality was huge here, that a lot of the cost went toward guaranteed discretion."

"You thought right." He slanted her a quick look. "Is there something you need to have kept quiet?"

"Me? No, but that woman from housekeeping…?"

"Ivy. She's been with me from the day we opened our doors."

"Then why would she mention a guest's name, Mr. Daniels, and associate it with the word 'problem'?"

She honestly expected Jack to be a bit annoyed by her question, by her pointing out his staff member's obvious faux pas. But he surprised her by saying, "There is no Mr. Daniels. At least, not right now."

She didn't understand. "But she said—"

"She said there's a problem and Malone is following up on it. The name, Mr. Daniels, isn't a guest's name, but it names a guest's problem."

She frowned at him, and when he turned to meet her gaze before looking back at the road ahead of them, she could have sworn he was challenging her to figure it out. And suddenly she understood. "Oh, Daniels, as in Jack Daniel's?"

"Bingo. Give the lady a cigar."

She should have known. Neither he nor his staff would ever breach confidentiality like that. "So, you have a guest—?"

"Guests, a couple."

"Guests who did too much celebrating and it's become a problem?"

"You said it. I didn't."

"And Malone, that gentle giant, is taking care of the detox?"

He chuckled softly. "Gentle giant? Sure, why not. He's just doing his job."

She looked away from Jack and out at the land around them. It was more raw up here, fewer buildings. In fact, she hadn't seen a building for a while, but, then again, they could be there hidden by the heavy snow. It had snowed again last night, and there was little evidence that anyone was up here, aside from the blade marks of a plow that had pushed snow into six-foot-high piles to either side of the blacktop.

"What is his job, exactly?" she asked.

Jack didn't miss a beat. "Everything. Anything. When he hired on, there wasn't a job description for him. The closest would be my personal assistant, but that sounds more limited than it actually is."

A man who delegated. A man who trusted Malone. She had a feeling that when Jack left, Malone would have a lot more power.

He startled her when he suddenly asked, "Are you married?"

"No, I'm not."

"Divorced?"

"No, and no significant other," she responded, wanting to end this line of questioning. She diverted it with, "I heard you're leaving town. Word is you've got some woman waiting for you at some fancy island resort."

He slowed the car, turned left onto a road that had been cleared, but only to give passage to one car at a time. "You heard that?" he finally said.

"Yeah. Word is you're heading out to meet up with some mysterious woman, and then you're taking off to an island or someplace to…" Her voice trailed off. "To do whatever."

She'd halfway thought he'd laugh at that, but he didn't. "I'm leaving town for an indefinite period of time, that's true. But I'm leaving alone, and there's no one waiting for me." He said the words in a flat tone that jarred something in her, but before she could figure it out, he said, "Gossip is one of our top products in the area." He chuckled, but there didn't seem to be a lot of amusement in the sound. "Too bad we can't use it as an export and make some money on it."

He was probably the prime target of gossip. No, she *knew* he was. Yesterday when she'd wandered through The Inn, trying to see what she could and taking some pictures, she'd heard whisperings about "the boss" along the way. What she'd told him was pretty darn close to what she'd heard. She'd just cut out the "He's got women falling at his feet, and when he heads down to Las Vegas, he and Cain Stone party." Now, she'd been told, Cain Stone, the owner of the Dream Catcher Casino and Hotel, and one of Jack's best friends, was getting married. The general consensus was "the boss doesn't like it." She wondered why he didn't like it.

"You'd be even richer, wouldn't you?"

She watched him, and didn't miss the way his hands tightened on the steering wheel as the car slowed more and more. She didn't have any idea why anything anyone said about him would matter at all. Nor why he was leaving. She'd like to find out—she wanted to make sure there weren't problems with The Inn or with the area.

He cast her a quick glance, and the subject came right back to her with a thud. "Not married, not divorced, not involved. What's with the ring?"

She instinctively touched the wedding band on her right hand, felt the cool smoothness of the gold with the tips of her fingers. "It was my mother's," she said, and wasn't going to go any further with the explanation. Instead, she looked around at the snow-covered land, at the massive trees and the peaks of the mountains thrusting into the sky so far that clouds clung to them. "You know, this is wonderful country."

"Yes, it is," he said, and didn't pry any more deeply into her reasons for wearing the ring. "The morning you saw me skiing, I came from up here. It never ceases to amaze me." The plowed snow at the sides of the road buried the trunks of the towering pines for at least the first eight feet.

"This is the mountain you own?"

"For now."

"They say you're selling it." That wasn't true. No one had talked about land sales, just about the man himself.

"Oh, they do, do they?"

"You aren't?"

"I might let it go."

"Why?"

He shrugged, the action tugging at his heavy jacket. "Business."

That told her nothing at all, but she didn't push. Instead, she asked him something she really was curious about. "Where are you going when you leave if it isn't to an island hideaway with a mysterious woman?"

He flashed a grin at her, a decidedly boyish expression that made something around her heart catch. "Geez, it makes me wish that's what I was going to do," he said.

"No chance of the island and the woman?"

"Never say never," he answered vaguely as he watched the road ahead.

"So it's a possibility?"

He chuckled again, but this time she could hear amusement in the sound. She liked it. "What is this, the Inquisition? Keep up, bit by bit, and I'll spill my guts?"

"I don't peg you as a man who spills his guts to anyone."

"Not usually," he murmured. "And you don't give up, do you?"

"Not usually," she parroted. "But, for you, I'll give up."

"Thanks," he said.

He turned left again and she suddenly realized that they had made a huge U-turn and were heading south again. The road narrowed even more now, and she could feel the big car labor a bit at the climb. They passed so close to the piled snow on the road sides that if she put her hand out the window, she would touch the icy crystals. Then there was snow piled on only one side, and to the other, the land fell away. She now had a panoramic view of the valley.

Almost as quickly as it had been exposed, the view was gone, and they were cutting back into the land. Jack came to a stop, and she realized why. The road ahead was nonexistent. Snow was everywhere, shrouding the land in its whiteness, giving only hints at the trees and ground it covered. A huge mound of snow pushed by the plows blocked the road completely.

"We're here," he said, and turned off the car.

She looked around again, but couldn't see any sort of building at all. "Where is here?"

He pushed open his door and cold air rushed into the car. "Come on, and I'll show you the scene of the infamous wine barrel incident." He grinned that grin, and she felt her breath catch. "Coming?"

"You bet," she said, and opened her own door, grabbed the strap and lowered herself to the ground.

She tucked her chin into the collar of her jacket to protect against the biting cold. She trudged around to the front of the car and met Jack there. "Okay, where did you do it?"

"We're going to have to hike a bit."

"No problem. Just lead the way."

He looked down at her for a long moment, then exhaled a breath that curled into the air between them. "Are you for real?" he asked softly.

"Excuse me?"

"You aren't going to ask me to get someone to clear a path for you?"

She smiled. "No, and I don't need someone to bring me hot chocolate at the moment. Although, it does sound rather wonderful."

She was trying to make light of things, trying to keep this on an even keel. She knew, deep down, that she was safe with Jack if she didn't allow this little excursion to be more than a tour of his mountain. But she just never counted on him smiling at her, touching her chin with his forefinger and saying, "Damn it, I like you, Jillian O'Shay."

Chapter Five

For one terrifying moment, Jillian was certain he'd kiss her again, without the music, without the celebration around them, without the excuse of it being New Year's Eve. His gaze lowered to her lips, lingered, then met her eyes again. Oh, no! She had a job to do and she was standing there wondering about him kissing her. Thankfully, he didn't come closer. "Now, the big reveal," he said, and stepped away.

She stood there without moving until she felt the air go back into her lungs. Jack had turned, and she watched him head toward something she hadn't noticed until then. There was a slight indentation in the snow back by the car. Although the new snow had partially filled it in, she could see that it was heading away from the car and into a stand of massive pines that quite literally groaned from the weight of the snow on them.

She stared at Jack as he climbed the bank, then turned to look down at her. Damn it, why did he have to be so...so... What? Sexy? Endearing? Fascinating? No, tempting. That was it. Tempting. Her fear grew as he crouched and held his hand out to her to help her up the bank. She would have ignored the help if she could have gotten up there without his assistance. She couldn't, so she reached out and let his fingers close around hers. He pulled her up easily. She steadied herself, then drew back and out of his hold.

She saw a small clearing beyond where they stood, and past that were dense trees that seemed to form a broad U around the spot. Jack went first down the other side of the bank and she followed. When she got to the bottom, she sank into the snow up to her knees. Jack started out for the trees and called over his shoulder to her, "Keep in my tracks and it won't be so hard."

She did what he said, and they made it to the dense stand of pines. She followed Jack into the trees, and the silence there was complete, except for the crunching of the snow when they stepped.

Then Jack ducked under a low branch, and she lost sight of him. But his voice found her. "Come on," he called back.

She stayed in his tracks, went under the branch, and stepped up and out into another clearing. But this place looked as if it were the edge of the world. The land fell away and all she could see was the grayness of the darkening sky dead ahead. Jack was on the edge. He turned to face her and motioned with one hand for her to go to him. When she reached him, she saw they were on an outcropping that hung out over the world below.

"Oh, my," she breathed. "This is incredible."

Far below was The Inn. It looked like some miniature set that someone had fashioned for them. Small buildings, larger buildings, wisps of smoke curling into the sky from rock chimneys. She couldn't see people, but there was a car on the road beyond it, heading south. It looked like a toy she could just bend over and pick up.

"It is, isn't it?"

No wonder Ray's people had made this parcel their first choice in the area. The idea of a development with a view like this, and ski runs that would make any skiing afficionado drool, made this land perfect. She gazed down at the town and resort. "Whose was this before?"

"An old-timer in the town, Scott Jennings. He died and his heir sold it to me."

"And you're going to sell it?"

"Possibly." Ray hadn't told her he had any reservations about the sale, unless he was being coy in the hopes of getting a higher price for it. "I'm considering my options."

"Such as?"

He squinted into the distance. "I'm not sure."

She looked in the same direction. "So, where is it?" she asked.

"It?"

"The site of the infamous wine barrel test."

He grinned at her, and looked so appealing that she had to avert her gaze. "Right about here," he said, "then over and off, and on down the slope." He motioned to the left, down the drop, and she went a bit closer to the edge. "The offending tree is that weird pine that looks as if it's been split in two. A lightning strike caused that. My impact didn't."

It was indeed a weird-looking pine, quite literally divided in two, as if a huge ax had been used on it. "How in the heck, if you started here, did you end up over there?"

"I don't know. I was in the barrel, and by the time I came around after the impact, I couldn't remember what happened."

She could almost see the wild flight of a wine barrel with a kid in it crashing into the tree. She barely suppressed a shudder. "You're lucky to be alive." She shifted her gaze to the scenery far below. "Why would you want to leave this place?" she asked.

"I need a change."

"What more could you want than to have this every day?"

"I don't know," he said, his voice a mere whisper, and when she turned to him, the look on his face surprised her. His lips were tight, and his eyes were narrowed. "That's what I plan to find out."

There was such emptiness in his tone that Jillian moved back a pace. She didn't want to feel this man's loneliness. She didn't want to have an impulse to touch him, make some sort of physical contact. And so she turned abruptly and said words that sounded hollow to her as they hung in the air between them. "I hope it works for you."

She started back the way they'd come, hurrying along the path they'd cut in the new snow, and she didn't have to look behind to know Jack was following her. She felt him near her back. She felt him close when she broke out of the trees at the flat spot and headed to the road. She felt him when she climbed the bank, scrambling to make it back up and over to get to the car. But he didn't touch her or offer to help her. She jumped down on the other side, went to the car and opened her door.

She was in before Jack got behind the wheel. She didn't have to look to know his eyes were on her. She didn't meet his gaze. Instead, she took her time doing up her seat belt, then she heard him shift and do the same right before he started the car. Heat flooded the interior, and it made her tremble for a moment. Then Jack eased the car back, did a tight turn and started back down the way they'd come.

Jillian stared straight ahead and suddenly caught a flash of movement from the left. The next instant, a deer bounded out of the snow into the path of the car. She heard her own "Oh, no!" at the same instant Jack braked hard. The car grabbed, shook, then the deer bounded in front of them and leapt into the space where the drop off came. It looked as if the animal had jumped into nothingness.

"Oh, my gosh," she gasped, a hand pressed to her chest as she turned to Jack. "It got away."

Jack looked at her, then the world shifted. No, not the world, the car. It started to lean oddly toward her side, as if Jack's side was being lifted into the air by an unseen hand. Time slowed to a painful crawl as it went higher and higher in tiny increments. She grabbed for Jack, catching his jacket sleeve, but it didn't do any good. "What…?" The car kept lifting, then with a horrendous shudder, she felt it start to slide toward the void where the deer had disappeared.

Jack had driven these hills since he'd been fourteen and he and Cain had taken his dad's truck for more than one joyride. He'd had deers blindside his car, and he'd survived. When he'd seen the flash to his left, he'd known it was a deer before he'd actually seen the doe leap onto the road, right in their path. He braked before he thought and he jerked at the wheel, hoping to avoid hitting the deer.

He expected an impact of some sort, and when it didn't come, he let out a sigh of relief—until he understood what had happened. He'd gone too close to the edge, sliding into the snowbank, and when the car started to tilt toward the bank, he knew that the piled snow hadn't been entirely on the road. Or the asphalt was giving way from the weight of the car. Whatever it was, the car was tipping to his right, slowly but inevitably.

Jillian had him by the arm, all the while screaming to make it stop. God, he wished he could. He yelled at her to hold on, and waited for the flip to come, that moment when the car's weight pulled it in a roll over itself, but amazingly that didn't happen.

The slide went on for what seemed like forever. There were jolts, impacts, but none that stopped the slide. Then a crunching sound, a jerk that pulled his seat belt strap deep into his shoulder, then suddenly all movement stopped with them almost level. The disturbed snow swirled all around them, then started to settle, and he realized that his hand was holding Jillian's hand. He had no idea when that had happened.

He inhaled, looked at her, saw the paleness of her face, the fear in her eyes. Then he looked beyond her and saw nothing but the plunge. He couldn't figure out what had stopped them. A huge tree. He didn't see any. A deep boulder. That would have caved in the side of the car. She clung to his hand so tightly his fingers were almost numb.

He had the oddest urge to laugh and never stop, to shout at the top of his lungs that they were alive, but any victorious celebrating was cut short when the car groaned and he felt it slip a bit, then stop again. No tree. No boulder. He knew then what had happened. They'd been stopped by a fire break road just below the rim. A roughly cut passage for firefighters in the event of a fire, and it had saved them from the plunge into the gorge.

"A fire road," he said, closing his eyes for a moment to try to stop the hammering of his heart. "We hit a fire road." He felt the trembling in her, and he turned to her again. "We're okay," he said. "We'll go and—" His words were cut off when the car started to move again, but it wasn't sliding. It was starting to tip the way it had initially. This time he didn't fool with the steering wheel or yell at her to hold on. If they went over this time, they wouldn't live to tell about it. There was nothing to stop their descent.

"Jillian," he said in a rush, "we have to get out." She didn't move. She just stared at him. "Get your seat belt undone, now!"

He undid his with one flip, then helped her undo hers. "Now get over here," he said, when the belt slid off of her. "Ease on over. Nothing sudden. Careful. Be careful."

"B-but I…"

"Now, Jillian! Now!" he said, and reached for her arm. If she hadn't moved on her own, he was going to drag her across the console and over to him. But she turned, reaching out with one hand to grip the steering wheel, the other hand grabbing a clump of his leather jacket. When she pulled, he got his right arm up and under hers and circled her waist to give her leverage. "Easy, easy," he breathed. "No sudden moves. Just ease on over."

She did as he said, then she was lying awkwardly in his lap, between him and the steering wheel. Her hair tickled his face and the scent of roses… He swallowed hard, held her to him with his arm around her waist and ignored the car when it slipped a bit more. He concentrated on getting his finger on the window button and pressed it to lower the glass.

He whispered, as if keeping his voice low would make the ground stay under the car for as long as they needed to get out safely. "We'll go out the window so we won't cause too much movement." The cold air came in a rush.

When she started to say something, he stilled her.

"Listen, you get out through the window and run like hell up the road. Get as far from the car as you can." He drew back enough to meet her gaze. "Do you understand?"

She started to shake her head, and he bit out, "Do it!"

Her lips worked, but nothing came. She finally nodded.

"Get out. Grab the door frame on both sides and pull. I'll push, and you dive out if you have to."

She hesitated, and he knew they didn't have time. He leaned toward her, getting his lips so close to her ear that he felt her skin against them. "Do it now or we'll die. Please."

She didn't hesitate further. She was moving, grabbing the window frame, pulling herself across him, and he caught her at the hips, helping her up and through. He felt her twist, then she said, "Let go," and he did. She was through the window, falling out of sight, then she was there at the window with snow clinging to her everywhere.

She reached her hand out to him. "Come on. Hurry!"

He wanted to yell at her to run, but sensing she'd ignore the command, he caught her hand, grabbed the window frame with his free hand and pulled hard. With her tugging on him, and his strength against the frame, he got out and free of the car. The two of them fell back into the snow, tangled in the coldness, and as he stumbled to his feet, he felt the earth start to tremble.

The fire road was at the most six feet wide, and the impact from the car had made it unstable. It was crumbling right out from under them. "Run!" he yelled as he grabbed Jillian and pulled her with him up the road. The deep snow made movement difficult, but he kept going, dragging her with him. Then he spotted a portion of heavy chain that he knew blocked access to the fire road at the top and he headed for it. He caught it with his free hand and used it as leverage to pull Jillian up to him.

He turned at the same time there was a low, unearthly groan from the earth, then as he held Jillian to him, they watched the car tip again with agonizing slowness. Suddenly the earth broke, and the car disappeared in a cloud of snow. Sounds echoed back to them, as the car bounced on the way down, then with a final crash and scream of ripping metal, the noises stopped.

Jack turned from the sight, gripped Jillian's hand and brought her with him over the chain, through the drift and finally up onto the road. With solid ground beneath him, he pulled Jillian into his arms. He held on to her tightly, letting it sink in that they were safe. That they hadn't died. That they were here, together.

She was shaking horribly, and he whispered over and over again, "We're okay." He closed his eyes so tightly that colors danced behind his lids. "We're okay. We're okay."

He let out a long, harsh breath of relief and gave silent thanks that they were up here and not down there. As he opened his eyes, he was aware of life all around him. Of the sway of the trees, the snow gleaming on the land, and Jillian in his arms.

He felt the heat of her body, felt every breath she

took, every ounce of life between them. It was as if he had refocused in some way. He saw life in all its glory. A reaction to the near miss, he was sure, but he couldn't stop the very real thought that his sense of euphoria and joy wasn't just because of his own survival, but because Jillian had survived, too. That she was here. That he was holding her. That they were safe.

It was then she seemed to still, and she eased back to turn a tear-streaked face up to his. She'd been crying. "We could have died," she whispered.

He touched her damp cheek and brushed at her tears. "We didn't. We didn't."

She looked around, then back at him, her blue eyes wide. "We…we need to call someone."

He wished they could. "My phone's in that car," he said.

She pulled back and he let her go, but he was poised to grab her if she crumbled. She certainly looked as if she might. But she reached in her pocket and took out a tiny cell phone. The picture phone Malone had told him about. She flipped it open, then groaned. "There isn't any signal." He grabbed the phone just before it tumbled out of her hand. "Malone, your assistant, he'll come looking for us, won't he?"

"No, he won't. He's used to me going off. He's not paid to keep tabs on me, unless I ask him to." He pushed his hands into his pockets along with her phone. "I never do that." He looked up and down the road and tried to figure out the best thing to do.

It was getting colder, and their clothes weren't

exactly survival wear. He knew how fast the cold could overtake a person up here. "I think we have two options," he said, but even as he said them, he knew they had only one. "We can walk down to the highway and try to hitch a ride from someone."

She'd never make it that far. He would, but he couldn't count on her being able to do it. And if he tried to carry her, neither would he make it. So he put out the only option that made sense. "Or we can go back up the way we came. Right where we parked, up an incline, there's a cabin that came with the land. We could go there, hope there's wood for a fire, then rethink what we can do. There might even be a phone on a landline up there. At the least, we'll be out of the cold."

"I don't know," she said, then shivered suddenly and hugged her arms around herself.

He took the choice out of her hands. "The cabin." He needed to get her inside, get some warmth going and let her catch her breath. They might still have to walk to the highway, but when they did, she'd be ready for it. "Let's go," he said.

Jillian wasn't at all sure she could walk, let alone uphill in this cold. The world seemed fuzzy for her, her thoughts jumbled and scattered. The only reality came when Jack put his arm around her shoulders, pulled her close to him and they started back up the hill together.

She let herself lean on him, let the feeling of him supporting her settle in her, and she tried as best she could to forget the crash and those moments when she thought they were going to die....

"Just a bit farther," he murmured when they reached the place they'd parked moments ago.

She squinted as he spoke, and thought how calm she'd been minutes before. She'd come to see the land. To see its potential and to see the place that Jack had done his wine barrel testing. A lifetime ago, she thought, and felt colder than she thought it was possible to be. She just hoped the cabin wasn't much farther. If it was, she wasn't sure she could make it.

Jack let go of her so he could climb the mound of snow to the right. He got to the top, then crouched and held out his hand to her, and memories of the moment he'd done the very same thing in the car, when he'd helped her up and through the window, into the snow, flooded her. His fingers were strong and warm, despite the pervasive chill. He pulled and she made it up and over the mound into the clearing again.

But instead of heading toward the dense pines, Jack turned right and made a new path through the calf-deep snow. He led the way and she realized that they were heading up a steep climb. Just when she thought she couldn't go any farther, he stopped. She got up beside him, and he said, "Just a few more feet and we're there. Okay?"

"Okay," she panted.

He went ahead, stomping his feet to crush down a path for her, then they crested the hill. "There it is," he said, and she made her way to his side to look up ahead at what she guessed was a small cabin, almost obliterated by snow.

She could see a chimney jutting from what she thought was a steep roof, and a few windows that peeked through the whiteness onto what was probably a porch. The snow had claimed it, too.

Jack headed for it, slowed, then kicked at the snow and she heard a connection with wood. Stairs. He kicked again, cleared a small part of one stair, then another, and when he got to the porch, he swung his booted foot in an arc, and snow flew out of the way.

He turned and looked down at her from the vantage point of the porch. "We made it," he said, and she just stared up at him. She couldn't even put one foot in front of the other now.

As if he read her mind, he came down to her, and in one easy motion he had her in his arms and was carrying her up the porch stairs. "Hold on," he said, and crossed the cleared spot on the porch and got to a weathered wooden door. "If you can reach over the jamb, see if the key's there?"

With one arm around his neck, she stretched out her other hand. She felt along the top of the doorjamb, and touched freezing metal. A key. She was afraid he'd ask her to put it in the lock, and she knew she couldn't. Her hands were too unsteady. Fortunately, he shifted, took it from her, and awkwardly managed to unlock the door. He kicked the barrier back with his foot and then they were inside.

She got an impression of old, worn furniture in a single room divided in two by a massive stone fireplace. A kitchen alcove was to the right, and she caught a glimpse of an old-fashioned iron bed on the other side of the hearth. Then Jack was crossing to a sagging couch, and he put her down on the worn cushions. He straightened to look down at her for a long moment before he went to the fireplace. "There's wood and there are matches, so I'll get a fire going, then we can figure out what to do," he said over his shoulder to her.

She didn't move. She simply sat there watching Jack crouch in front of the hearth and start to build a fire. He worked quickly, efficiently, as if he'd been doing it all his life, then he finally straightened and took off his jacket. He tossed it on the hearth before he came back to where she sat, then hunkered down in front of her, coming to her eye level. "Are you okay?"

She wanted to say she was, but she couldn't even make her lips work to form the words. She knew if she tried to speak, she'd start crying again and she hated that. She wasn't a crier. Never had been. No matter what. But tears were very close to the surface again right then. He didn't even wait to see if she could undo her jacket, just reached toward her and undid the fastenings. Then he eased it off her shoulders and let it fall to the couch behind her.

Next, he lifted her right foot, tugged off the boot, then did the same with the other foot. "I'm going to see if there's coffee," he said, but he didn't make a move to go and do it.

She realized he was uncertain about leaving her there while he went a simple eight feet away. She must look awful, as if she were ready to fall apart. She was on the verge of losing control. "I…I'm okay," she managed to croak in a voice that sounded like someone else's.

He hesitated, then touched her cheek with his hand. Her skin was like ice. His was like fire. She trembled from the contact and couldn't stop. He didn't go to the kitchen area. Instead, he got up and sat on the couch beside her, then pulled her into the curve of his arm. She let her head fall against his shoulder.

Chapter Six

Jack didn't speak. He just held her. And gradually the connection started to work for Jillian. The trembling lessened and her mind seemed to clear. They were alive. Period. She didn't believe in what-ifs—they solved nothing. She'd learned that with her dad. Take what you can, and don't dwell on what might have been. They were stuck in this cabin, but they were alive.

Jack spoke near her ear, close enough for her to feel the warmth of his breath. "Better?"

"Better," she said, and meant it. This wasn't insurmountable. It was doable. Being at the bottom of the canyon would have been insurmountable.

"Good," he said, and the connection was broken when he got to his feet and headed to the kitchen.

She sank back into the cushions of the couch, the fire warming her face, and stared at the flames growing stronger with each passing moment.

"Coffee," Jack called to her. "Even some tea, if you'd rather have that? It's not green, but it's tea."

She looked over at him, and he was watching her. Clearly he still wasn't sure if she was going to stay calm. "Tea would be wonderful," she said in as steady a voice as she could muster.

She curled up in a corner of the couch, tucking her feet under her. The heat from the fire was luxurious, even if it made her face and hands throb slightly. She watched Jack move around the small space by the cupboards. There was the clatter of dishes, then a whistle blew, making Jillian jump.

"Sorry," Jack said. "I didn't expect the kettle to whistle."

She settled back as Jack poured hot water in large mugs, then put a teabag in one and instant coffee in the other. "I can't find any cream or sugar," he said, carrying both mugs over to the couch. "Or honey or lemon."

She didn't care. He handed one to her, then took a seat on the couch by her, stretching his legs out toward the fire and setting his mug on his thigh. "This isn't the way I thought today would go," he murmured.

She actually laughed. It surprised her to be laughing so close to the horror of the accident. "Me, neither," she said, and cupped the mug in both hands, letting the warmth seep into her.

He cast her a glance, probably wondering if she was getting hysterical. "You know, you surprise me," he said.

"Me? How?"

"Most women in your position would be either having a tantrum about the mess, or they'd be threatening to sue me, or they'd be passed out cold."

She laughed again, and it was easier this time. "I'm not given to tantrums or suing people, and the last time I passed out…" The words died off at the same rate as her humor. She remembered that she'd fainted right after her mother had died. She jerked back to the present, leaving the past in its place. "I don't do that very often."

He studied her. "I bet you don't get in accidents like that very often, either."

"Never," she said, and tugged the string for the teabag. She watched the liquid get darker, then she left the bag in the mug and took a sip. The hot tea was wonderful, warming her on its way down and easing something in her. "I never tried to go down a ski run in a wine barrel, either." She drank more tea. "Ah," she sighed with pleasure. "This is terrific."

He wasn't laughing, not even smiling. "I can't believe we walked away."

She sobered at that. "My dad always said, if it's your time, it's your time. Period. If it's not, get up and get going, because you've got more life to live."

He smiled slightly at her words, an upward curve of his lips at the corners. "I think your dad sounds pretty smart," he said in a low voice, then turned and drank some of his coffee.

He had been smart. He'd been bright and funny and wise. It seemed like a long time ago, now. "He was."

He cast her a slanting glance. "Was? I'm sorry, I—"

"No, no, he's not dead. He's just…he hasn't been

well, and he's different than he used to be." That sounded so simple, when it really wasn't at all.

Thank goodness he didn't say he was sorry or how sad that was. He just sipped more coffee and stared at the fire. "People change," he murmured. "And people surprise me."

She studied him openly, and wanted to say he surprised her. He made coffee. He made tea. He wasn't standing on the road, waiting for some assistant or some flunky to make his life easier. He was doing that himself. "Any ideas what to do now?" she asked.

"I told you that no one will be looking for me." He eyed her from under partially lowered lids. "Will anyone be asking about you? Wondering where you are today?"

She shook her head. Ray wouldn't try to contact until tonight, if he did at all. Her few friends knew she was gone for at least a week. "No, no one."

"How about your father?"

She'd never wanted to talk about Johnny with strangers, but with Jack, the subject came up more than it had with anyone for a very long time. For some inexplicable reason, she wanted to tell Jack about her dad. "My dad…" She bit her lip. "I told you he's not well, but it's a bit more complicated than that. He's…" Why couldn't she just say it? What difference would it make? "He needs a lot of one-on-one care." He wouldn't even know she was gone. "He wouldn't be looking for me."

He was quiet for a long moment. "What about your mother?"

"She died when I was in college." She didn't wait for

him to say the usual "I'm so sorry" or "I didn't know." Of course he wouldn't know. "What about your parents? Where are they?"

He took a long drink of his coffee, then shifted toward her, resting one arm on the back of the couch. "They prefer Switzerland to here. They prefer their friends there. They prefer the 'ambience' there. I heard that all the time, and thought I knew what it meant, but from them, it's pig Latin. Just a way of saying they want to be left alone to do their own thing. They want a place where the attitude is 'I don't know you, and whatever you do or whatever you are is none of my business.' As opposed to Silver Creek, where everything is everyone's business."

"That sounds really cold."

He looked at her, then laughed at her choice of words. "Well, Switzerland *is* damn cold," he finally said.

She found herself laughing in response, saying, "Cold, really damn cold," and barely able to get the words out. The laughter took on a life of its own, and at some point it changed from amusement, to almost hysteria. She couldn't stop and when the tears rolled down her cheeks, she couldn't stop them, either.

Jack wasn't laughing. He was watching her, then saying, "It's not that funny," until he finally dropped his arm to her shoulders and pulled her against his side. Her face pressed into his chest, and his voice seemed to surround her. "It's okay. It's okay."

Jack knew that things had gone over the edge for Jillian when he saw the huge tears start to roll down her cheeks. He pulled her to him, not knowing what else to do. She was in shock obviously, and she needed to feel safe and be warm—and well away from where the accident happened. He needed to get them both back to The Inn as soon as he could. No more talks about their parents. He wouldn't think about why he'd been able to put all the years of tension between him and his parents into a few sentences for Jillian that encapsulated their attitudes perfectly.

He rubbed her back and whispered, "We'll be back at The Inn before you know it."

He thought she whispered, "Thank you," but he wasn't sure if it was that or just a sigh. He stared over her head at the fire, felt its heat and the heat that was coming from Jillian. He inhaled that rose scent, felt her softness in his arms, and he was taken aback by the sudden realization that it felt right. *He* just felt right. This quiet, Jillian, someone to hold on to. Being with her, no matter what had happened.

As the minutes passed, he marveled that until now, he'd felt that Silver Creek had nothing more for him. That his only connection here was his handful of good friends. That Silver Creek was a place he'd rather not be. Home or not, he'd been going to leave. To put everything behind him. But in that moment, he realized he wasn't quite as anxious to leave as he had been earlier. He was going to leave, that was a given, and it would be soon, but maybe he'd be around a few more days than he'd thought he would be.

She shifted and he reluctantly let her go. She settled back in the cushions, slipping low to rest her head against the back of the sofa and stare up at the ceiling. Her lashes were spiked with tears, and he saw the way her hands nervously swiped at her cheeks before being clasped together tightly on her stomach. "I'm sorry," she said. "That won't happen again."

He wasn't so sure he wanted that promise from her. Take away the panicked hysteria, and holding Jillian O'Shay had its good points. Hell, it had *more* than good points. He sat forward, put his coffee on the floor by the sofa, then looked back at her. He let himself brush at a wisp of hair at her temple and felt the silkiness of her skin. Then he turned and copied her, slouching low, resting his head on the cushions and thrusting his feet out in front of him.

"What now?" she asked softly.

He stared at the flames leaping in the fireplace. What now, indeed? "I'm going to walk to the highway to get help." He pushed himself to his feet. "You stay here and I'll be back soon," he said as he crossed to the hearth to get his jacket.

He shrugged it on, and when he turned, Jillian was by the door putting on *her* jacket. "I'm going, too."

"No, no, you don't have to," he said, crossing the small cabin to where she stood. "Wait here. Stay warm."

She hesitated, then frowned slightly. "I don't want to."

Was this the moment a spoiled rich girl appeared and tore apart his opinion of her? "I want you to."

She didn't budge. "I don't want to." Before he could argue, she said quickly, "I don't want to stay here alone."

"I won't be gone long."

"How do you know?" He looked down at her as she fumbled with the fasteners on her jacket. She wasn't looking at him now, intent on doing up the garment, but she kept talking. "You never thought your car would be at the bottom of the gully, did you? Or that we'd barely get out before it fell." That was when she lifted her gaze to his, her blue eyes intent on him. "I'm not staying here alone."

He gave up. "Okay, let's go," he said, and reached for the door at the same moment he thought he heard someone calling his name.

He jerked the door open and looked out. In the midst of the glistening white of the snow, he saw a flash of color, maybe green, he wasn't sure. Then he was certain.

There *was* someone at the rise, breaking into view, a man with his hands cupped to his mouth shouting, "Jack! Jack!" then lifting a hand in a wave. "Got him!" he shouted to whomever was behind him.

"Charley?" Jack called out. "Is that you?"

"Damn straight it's me," Charley shouted as he approached the cabin using the trail Jack and Jillian had made earlier. "You're a sight for sore eyes, boy," the heavyset man in his sheriff's jacket and hat said. "You had us all royally scared when we found the car and knew no one could have survived that fall. Thank God Todd spotted your tracks at the fire road."

He was close to the porch now. He looked up and

stopped. "I *thought* there were two sets of tracks," he said, squinting up at Jillian.

"Jillian," Jack said, "this is Charley. He's what passes for the law around here."

Charley grinned. "Yeah, I do pass for that," he said, climbing the porch steps. "You two tumbled to the fire road?"

"Yeah, we did. We barely got out before the road gave way and took the car with it."

"You're the luckiest son of a gun I've ever seen."

"We were very lucky," Jack concurred, and for some reason he found himself putting an arm around Jillian's shoulder. He needed to hold her then, and he didn't question it. "But we're okay. We were just getting ready to head to the highway."

"No need. I've got a real serviceable squad car just down the way. Everyone's going to be pretty darn relieved that you're in one piece."

"How did you even know there was trouble?"

"We got a call from that security company that tracks cars, that built-in system that goes off when something happens? They said they had a signal that your air bags were deployed, and they gave us a rough idea where the car was. Todd and me came on up, and figured if you were around here, you'd be up this way, since you just bought the property and all."

Jack had forgotten about the security setup for the car. He was certainly grateful for it now. "We came to look over the land, and a deer almost blindsided us. The next thing we knew, we were sliding down to the fire road, then the road started to crumble."

Jillian spoke up then. "Jack got us out just in time."

"Well, ma'am, I think you're both pretty damn lucky."

"Yes, sir," she said quietly.

Charley didn't ask any questions about Jillian at all. He simply asked if they could make it to the squad car, and if they could, he'd be happy to chauffeur them back to The Inn. Jillian pulled away from Jack then and went back into the cabin. Jack saw her go to the fireplace, pick up their mugs and take them to the kitchen area, then rinse them out and start to put things away.

"Jillian, you don't have to—"

"Yes, I do," she said, and kept working.

Jack glanced back at Charley. "I'll be right there," he said, then went after Jillian. He quickly banked the fire. When he stood up and turned, Jillian was already by the door. They went out, and he locked up before Charley led the way through the snow to his car.

Going downhill on foot was a lot easier than going up, and they were back at the scene of the accident in moments. Two squad cars were parked near the gouge in the snow on the edge of the drop, and a tow truck was off to one side. Two men were peering over the edge of the drop-off. They turned when they heard the three of them approaching, and one of them—Rollie, the owner of the town's original garage—yelled, "Holy cow, Jack, you had us all looking for your pieces at the bottom of the drop." He hurried over to Jack and stopped just short of pulling him into a hug. "Damn glad you're okay." He smiled at Jillian. "And you, too. You were in the car with Jack?"

"Yes, I was."

Charley spoke up. "I'm taking them back so Gordie can check them out." He headed for the nearest squad car, saying over his shoulder, "You two. Come on." He got in behind the wheel, the engine roared to life and Jack opened the front passenger door for Jillian. Then he climbed into the back.

"Feel like old times?" Charley asked as he caught Jack's eye in the rearview mirror.

"It's been a while," Jack replied, and saw Jillian turn to glance at him.

"You've been in the back seat of a police car?" she asked.

While Charley maneuvered the car to head back down to the highway, he chuckled. "He's been back there quite a few times."

He saw Jillian smile as she looked at Charley. "Were you there when he did the wine barrel dare?"

Charley guffawed at that. "You know about that?"

"A bit. He claims he made it down, finally."

"Yeah, he made it down," Charley said with another glance back at Jack. "I bet he didn't tell you that one of his mistakes was hitting a tree."

"He told me about the tree," she said. "In fact, he showed it to me. I just wondered what he had to do to make it all the way down in one piece."

Charley laughed again. "Oh, he was ingenious. He

pushed a lot of stuffing into his clothes to pad himself, then took off. He made it down, and when they got him out of the barrel, he was in total misery."

She flashed a glance back at Jack, then at Charley. "Misery? He said he made it. He didn't say he hurt himself."

"Oh, he didn't break a leg or gash his head like he did when he hit the tree. Nothing like that, no blood, no broken bones." Charley was enjoying this far too much.

"Charley, that's all in the very distant past," Jack interjected.

"No, no, tell me what happened," Jillian insisted. She could tell that Charley was all too glad to tell her, and she wanted to know. It took her mind off the past few hours and off the tightness in her middle from just being in a car again. She needed a distraction so she didn't notice the way the road went into what seemed like sharp turns, or the drop to her right when she least expected it. "What did he use to pad himself in the barrel?"

"The dumb kid used fiberglass insulation for the stuffing. So, everywhere it touched him, the fiberglass cut into his skin. He was in misery for a week, at least."

"Oh," she said, looking at Jack.

He studied her for a long moment, then said, "You know, you have the remarkable ability to make that single little word so damned annoying."

"What little word?"

"Oh."

"Oh," she said, then found a real smile in her. "Oh."

Charley turned at the highway and they were on their way south toward The Inn. "You've been around here before?" he asked Jillian.

"This is my first stay at The Inn."

"You and Jack are old friends?"

"No," they both said at once. She didn't look back at Jack as she elaborated. "I'm staying at The Inn, and he was giving me a tour of the high country. We were on our way back when…." She bit her lip hard.

"If you'd been five feet farther in either direction, you'd never have made the fire road like you did."

That made her press back into the seat and wrap her arms around herself. Charley reached over and patted her arm. "Hey, you made it. That's what counts. Miss by an inch, miss by a mile, that's what I always say."

She still felt unnerved, and she forced herself to breathe deeply. "We made it," she said, and exhaled. She wasn't going to fall apart, not again, not here, and not now. They were almost at The Inn. Once they were there, she could go to her room and scream if she wanted to. But not now.

They got to the front gates, Charley drove through and Jack said, "Go around to the side, Charley."

"You got it," the man said, and pulled the car up to the side entrance. He twisted in the seat to talk to Jack directly. "I'll call you when we figure out what we're going to do about the car. Rollie seems to think he can get the car up. I'm thinking it should stay there and be a planter in the spring."

"I don't care," Jack said as Jillian opened her door.

"Thank you so much for finding us," she said to Charley.

He touched the tip of his cap and gave her smile. "Glad to do it. Glad to do it."

She was out in the cold, then Jack was there, taking her arm and waving to Charley. "Come on," he said, and took her to the side entrance and back to an elevator. He put in a code, the door slid back and he was about to lead her into the car when she asked, "This goes to my floor?"

"No, to my suite."

No, no, no. She couldn't do that. She wouldn't. She needed to be in her own space, not in *his* space. She shook her head. "I just want to go to my suite."

He didn't argue, thank goodness, but said, "Sure," and they walked through the lodge. Jack stayed close, but didn't take her arm again. Ivy, the housekeeper, saw them, and Jack motioned her over. They didn't stop walking and the woman fell in step with them. "Call the doctor and tell him I need to see him right away. I'll be in Miss O'Shay's suite."

"Yes, sir," she said, but didn't ask any questions. She just hurried off to do as he asked.

"I don't need a doctor," Jillian said as they went into the corridor that led to the north wing.

"You need to be checked out, just to be safe, okay?"

No, it wasn't okay. It wasn't okay to be here, to let him take care of her, to tell him about her dad or hear about his parents. It wasn't okay for her to feel herself falling into a place where he seemed to be her anchor.

She was here to spy on him, for heaven's sake. She didn't belong here. And she didn't belong with him. She just wanted to get to her room. The elevator was there, and she pushed the call button. She looked at Jack. "I'd thank you for the tour, but…" She tried to smile, but her mouth wouldn't form the expression.

The elevator was there, the doors sliding open, and when she got in, Jack went with her. "You don't have to come up with me."

"I know," he said, but hit the third-floor button and stood by her on the ride up.

When they got to the door to her suite, she pushed her hand in her jacket pocket, and her card wasn't there. She tried every pocket in her jacket and in her jeans. Not only was her security key card gone, but her phone was gone, too. "Oh, shoot," she muttered, realizing they could have come out of her pocket anywhere. In the car, on the road, in the cabin, in the police car. "My card's gone and so is my phone."

Jack reached into his pocket and took out a card. He inserted it in her door and pulled the handle. The door swung open. "You had my card?" she asked.

"No, it's a master for all the rooms, but—" he reached in his jacket pocket and took out her phone "—I do have this."

She remembered when she'd tried to use it and there hadn't been any signal. She couldn't remember Jack taking it, but was thankful she had it back and he hadn't seen the pictures on it that she still had to download.

"Thanks," she said, taking it from him. The metal casing was warm from his body heat. She went inside and turned, ready to figure out what to say to Jack before he left, but he had other ideas. The man was bent on being there, and she didn't have the energy to argue when he came into the room with her.

She simply crossed to a chair, took off her jacket and dropped it over the back, then sank into the couch in the sitting area. When she used her right hand to push herself back into the softness, she felt pain shoot down it. She flexed her arm and grimaced when more pain came. Jack stood over her, talking, asking her things, but she could barely concentrate or focus. She suspected that he'd seen her grimace, or maybe she'd gasped at the pain and hadn't realized it. Whatever, he was saying something about "Gordie," whoever that was, and his being "so damned slow."

Her thinking was getting fuzzy, and she rested her head on the back of the couch. She heard Jack move in the room, then the door clicked, and she thought he'd finally left. But the next moment, she heard another voice, a man's voice, someone she didn't know at all. She forced herself to open her eyes, and Jack was there with a tall man by his side. The stranger looked bulky in heavy outer clothes, and when he skimmed off a fur hat, she could see he was partially bald. He also had the kindest-looking brown eyes behind rimless glasses and a sweet smile when he hunkered down in front of her.

"I'm the doctor. You can call me Gordie. Everyone does. Jack told me about the accident. I'm just going to check you out, and make sure there isn't any damage."

He had a small flashlight in his hand, checked her eyes, then he was taking her pulse. "No blood, no scrapes, no abrasions." He sat back. "So far, so good."

He took a while to look at her right shoulder and declared, "It's an ugly bruise from the seat belt restraint," then he gave her something for the pain, helped her get the two pills down with water and the next thing she knew, he was leaving.

She heard him talking to Jack and thought she heard something about a hangover, but she didn't even try to follow their conversation. She thought he might have tried to examine Jack, but she stayed on the couch, her head back, her eyes closed, and felt weariness wash over her.

Jack was near her. She could almost feel him when he moved. Then she felt a brush at her hair—his touch, achingly gentle. "Gordie said you'll sleep for a while, and if you need it, he can do X-rays at the clinic."

She opened her eyes when the phone rang, and before she could even think about getting to her feet to answer it, Jack had.

"Hello?"

There was a long pause, then Jack said, "Of course, she's right here," and he crossed to hand her the cordless phone. As she took it, he said, "It's for you. It's a person named Ray, and he seems to think I'm a bellhop."

She put the phone to her ear and said, "Ray?" but watched Jack go to the door, turn to her and mouth the word, "Later," then quietly slip out.

Chapter Seven

Jack headed back to his suite, but never got there. He was waylaid by Malone, who didn't mention the accident, but just said, "Glad you're back." With that, the big man told him that Mr. Daniels was out of control, and his girlfriend was asking that they call the guy's psychiatrist to advise them what to do with him. It took the rest of the day to get it sorted out, culminating in arrangements to get him to a private facility near Las Vegas so the man and his companion could detox.

By the time he left Malone to finalize the trip, it was almost ten in the evening. He bypassed the main part of The Inn, went up to his suite and put in a call to Jillian's room. The phone rang five times before she answered with a sleepy "Hello?"

He loved the soft seductiveness of sleep in her voice. "It's Jack. Sorry to wake you."

"No…no problem," she breathed softly over the line. "Those pills made me…kind of groggy."

It was then he realized he'd been about to ask her to

have a drink. A very late dinner. Or just see her. That was stupid. "I just wanted to find out how you're doing."

"My arm's sore, but it's not too bad." He closed his eyes when she sighed over the line, and felt his body tense. "How about you?"

"I'll live. That's more than I can say for the car."

He wanted her to laugh, but she sighed again. "That's too bad."

His body had a life of its own and Jack knew better than to think it was nothing. He asked something that probably wasn't any of his business at all. But that didn't stop him. "So, did you explain to Ray that I wasn't a bellhop?"

"Oh, Ray," she said. "He knows."

"Good. Who exactly is Ray?" he asked, without the ability at that moment to be more subtle.

There was silence, then another sigh. God, those sighs were playing havoc with him. "He called to let me know about a problem I had to see about."

That was vague enough. "A problem, or a *problem?*" he asked.

"My dad, I told you he's sick, and he had a bit of a setback."

"Are you leaving?"

"No, I'm not. He'll be fine. He's got good help."

He released a sigh of his own now, a sigh he recognized as relief that she was staying. "If you're going to be around tomorrow, do you have any plans for the day?"

"I've heard your spa is terrific and I might try it out."

"Good. Good. Do that." He didn't know what else to

say, so he stuck with the simplest thing possible. "Good night, Jillian."

"Good night," she echoed, and the line went dead.

JACK NEVER DREAMED, at least, he never remembered his dreams. But the past few nights he'd had some. He knew he had, but he couldn't pull out the details. That night he dreamed, and the details were vivid. He'd close his eyes and he'd be in the car, tipping, going over, holding on to Jillian, hearing her screams, shooting out the side window, watching the car disappear. But the dreams didn't stop there. They didn't stop with him and Jillian making a run for it, getting to safety.

They skipped ahead, into a dream that wasn't part of the day. They were in the cabin, he and Jillian were in the bed with the fire roaring in the hearth, and he was kissing her. He was touching her, exploring her, and she touched him. He awoke suddenly, gasping, then pushing to sit up in his bed. He was alone in the dark, his breathing ragged, and he felt lonelier than he thought one person could feel.

With a low oath, he got out of bed, went in by the fire and had what brandy was left from his and Gordie's drinking bout the night before. He stared out into the night, and he didn't go back to bed until dawn started to break. He rolled onto his side, glanced out the windows and saw that snow was starting to fall. He grabbed his pillow, pushed his face into it and finally went back to sleep.

He didn't leave his suite until four o'clock that afternoon. He'd finally gotten some sleep, but was awakened by Malone and an urgent call from his attorney around eight. From then on, he'd been on the phone, wrestling with an idea that had been so very acceptable before New Year's Eve. The land. What he'd let go. The shedding of the pressures from his possessions. He had to make a decision now about what he'd sell and what he wouldn't. What sections he'd let go, and how quickly he'd make it happen. He'd been dead serious about doing it, as dead serious as he'd been about leaving town, but now he felt distracted. He couldn't concentrate, and making a decision wasn't coming easily to him.

He was waylaid by phone calls that had nothing to do with business, too. Cain called, saying he'd heard about the accident, and Josh called right after that. He rehashed the incident over and over again, and then Charley called to check on him. He made a limp joke about "Jack and Jill going down the hill," and Jack wasn't amused.

He finally handed the paperwork to Malone, told him to talk to the accountants and get the figures they needed. He wasn't taking any more phone calls, and he put off any more decisions, pushing his departure date back a few days. Then he headed out of the suite, went down to the main floor and heard himself being paged. "House phone, line twelve for Mr. Prescott."

He almost ignored it, but didn't. He grabbed the

nearest house phone and punched in twelve. It was Gordie wanting to know how he was doing. When he assured him he was just fine, Gordie asked about Jillian. "I don't know," Jack said. "I'll go and find out and let you know."

He hung up and knew that he'd come down to do that very thing. Find Jillian.

The Inn was alive today, unlike New Year's Day. Guests had fully recovered and were everywhere. He wandered through the rooms, stopping to talk to guests and staff, and through it all, he looked for Jillian. He found himself on the other end in the north wing, right by the elevator up to the third level. Coincidence? He wasn't going to fool himself. It was no coincidence at all. But when he went up to her suite, she didn't answer the door. He called the suite from a nearby house phone and got no answer. Then he remembered she'd mentioned having a day at the spa.

He went back down and instead of turning to go back into the main part of the lodge, he went in the opposite direction. The spa was in the same wing as Jillian's suite, all the way to the end and down a flight of stairs. He hurried along the corridor, then saw the archway that led to the bottom level. He took the stone steps two at a time and headed for a set of dark wooden doors. A discreet oval of brass was set in the stone wall by the doors and it read simply, The Spa at the Inn."

He pushed back the doors and stepped into the serene reception area. Here, rock and stone were replaced by polished and tumbled marble, and the colors were all pale pastels. Everything was smooth and elegant, subdued and restful. The fragrance of some exotic flower hung in the air, harp music was piped in from hidden speakers and glass shelves on either wall held displays of all the spa's creams and lotions blended exclusively for them.

The only deep color in the space was a single door to the right. It was glazed in a deep sapphire-blue and had a mirrorlike finish. The door moved as soon as Jack stepped in from the hallway, and the manager of the spa appeared.

Erica Swan. Jack had always thought the name was perfect for the tall, slender woman with the slightly sharp features, elegantly long neck and hair so blond it looked like platinum. She always wore tailored slacks and jackets in the same deep sapphire-blue as the door. "Mr. Prescott, welcome. How may I help you?" she asked as she met him in the middle of the space.

"I was looking for a guest, a Miss O'Shay."

"Of course, she's in the rock sauna. Do you want me to let her know you're here?"

"When will she be finished?"

Erica checked a slim watch on her wrist. "In fifteen minutes, unless she decides to do the facial. Would you like me to pass on a message?"

Fifteen minutes? "No, I'll just wait for her to finish."

"Since you're here, may I show you something?"

He had no interest in the workings of the spa as long

as it met the needs of his guests. "If you need to run something by someone, contact Malone and—"

She rolled her eyes with a "Please, spare me," expression, and said, "I think you're the one I need to run this past."

He didn't want to pull rank or tell her to leave him alone. He finally nodded. "Okay, what is it?"

"Let me show you in my office," she said, and turned to go back through the deep blue door. He had to either follow her or stay there and let her realize she was on her own. He followed.

They stepped into the main part of the spa. The marble flowed in and through to the hair salon, the massage rooms, the steam rooms and a gym that catered to people who were so obsessive about their workouts that they didn't take a vacation from them.

Erica went to a side door, pushed it and went in. Her office was white on white, even the marble was white. Her desk was little more then a piece of free-shaped glass perched on a series of stones and had nothing on it but a single phone and sapphire-blue bud vase that held a single white rose. "This is what I want you to see," she said, and he realized she'd picked up something from a side glass shelf. It was white and he hadn't noticed it set among the stacks of white towels.

She shook out what she had in her hand—it was a robe, a white, terry, plush, calf-length robe. An intricate monogram in the same sapphire-blue was over the heart, intertwined letters, a T and an I, over a single word, Spa. They used the robe at the spa and put them in the guest rooms.

"See this." Erica held it out in front of her by its shoulders, her nose wrinkled in what looked like disgust. "It's so…so wrong."

It looked fine to him. "What's wrong with it?"

"It's dated and ordinary. I think it needs to be updated. Maybe with gold piping on all the hems, and a gold belt." She wrinkled her nose again with dramatic distaste. "They look like every other robe in every other spa. We want to stand out." She smiled at him suddenly. "When people steal them, we want them to remember where they got them and be proud of them."

He wanted to laugh at that, but refrained, then glanced at his watch. Had it only been five minutes since he came through the doors of the spa? Erica obviously thought she'd lost him, because she spoke quickly. "The Inn is above all the other resorts, and we need to maintain a certain image."

Bottom line? He didn't care. If Erica thought it made the place better, he wouldn't argue. "Go ahead and make the change."

"Fantastic." A knock on the door caught her attention and she glanced past Jack. "Yes?"

He turned, and Ivy was in the doorway. "I'm sorry to be interrupting, but I'm looking for a guest, a Ms. O'Shay." She smiled at Jack. "I believe she was with you the other day when we had our conversation about Mr. Daniels?"

He remembered. "Is there a problem?"

"No, sir. She was talking to me earlier in her room, and she was so interested in the way we ran housekeeping that I said if she wanted a tour of our facility, I'd be glad to give her one." She frowned with a touch of concern. "I hope that's okay, sir. You always said to make sure the guest got everything they asked for. That is okay, isn't it?"

He always had said that, but he was at a loss to figure out why Jillian would show any interest in housekeeping beyond getting what she needed from them. "Of course, Ivy."

Her face cleared. "Good." She looked at Erica. "Where can I find her?"

"She's in the rock sauna. She should be out any minute."

Another voice was there outside the office, and this time Jack knew exactly who was there. "Oh, Ivy," Jillian said, and her voice came closer. Then she was there, by the tall woman, in one of the robes, with the terry spa slippers on her feet, and her hair swept up and off her face with a white headband. Her skin looked damp and flushed, and the blue of her eyes was just as blue as he remembered. Her hair curled wildly from the humidity.

Jillian felt her heart hammer against her ribs. Jack was there, not more than three feet from her, and she was standing by the housekeeper, feeling distinctly like an amateur at her job. Jack came closer, looking down at her, his eyes flicking over her from her feet to her head, then his gaze met hers. "How's the spa?" he asked without looking as if he thought there was anything odd about her wanting a tour of their housekeeping operations. Maybe the guests really did rule at The Inn, and nothing they asked for surprised him anymore.

She reined in her instant response that it was wonderful, one of the best small spas she'd been in. Instead, she said, "It's nice," and left it at that. He wouldn't expect someone who was supposed to be living around this sort of service all her life to be overly impressed. "I'll let you get back to business," she said, and would have turned to try to dig her way out of her agreement with Ivy, but Jack didn't let her.

"Wait. I came here looking for you," he said, and that made her heart rate speed up again. He came closer, diminishing any space they had between them. She felt Ivy step back, and she almost did, too, but stopped herself. Ivy was being subservient, and that wouldn't be expected of her. So she held her ground and tried to put on her best neutral expression.

"Me? Why?"

"I was checking on you for Gordie. He wanted to make sure everything was okay, and he didn't have the time to come all the way out here to do it himself."

That let her breathe a bit easier. "Oh, I'm just fine."

"That's good," he murmured, and she realized that not only was Ivy gone, but Erica was leaving by another door in the office.

"You…you're okay?" she said, and realized she had almost stammered the question.

Somehow she knew he knew that she wasn't exactly comfortable at that moment. "Oh, I'll live."

"I guess we both will," she managed. "Now I have to get dressed." With that she turned, feeling decidedly like an escapee, and so she made herself walk at a normal pace toward the back of the spa to the dressing rooms.

But she didn't escape. Jack was there by her, walking in step with her, and when she got to the door, she turned, forced a smile and pointed to the oval plaque of a lady's profile done in the deep sapphire-blue on the white door. "Unless you're planning on invading sacred space…?"

He smiled at her, and it made her own humor falter. Damn it, he had the best smile. It crinkled the corners of his eyes. He held out both hands, palms out. "Oh, no, of course not. I wanted to ask how your father is, too."

That made her tense. She'd been wrong to think that Ray wouldn't call her. He had done just that to tell her the care facility where her father lived had contacted him to let her know that Johnny had tried to get his wheelchair through the garden door and the whole chair had flipped over. He had a cut on his forehead, but otherwise was okay. Mixing all the worry over her father's fall with her own near miss in the car had made everything seem much worse.

Sleep had been hard to come by, and she'd decided, when she got back that she was going to make sure her dad had everything he needed if something happened to her. Ray knew a good law firm. She'd make sure she had good life insurance. It had seemed so simple during the night. But now, with Jack asking about him, she found her chest tightening.

"He had a fall, but it wasn't anything serious."

"Good." Jack motioned to the door to the dressing room. "Go ahead and get dressed. I'll wait."

"Wait?" she asked. He wasn't leaving? He wasn't going to say, "Well, it's been nice," and walk away?

He answered that completely. "The other reason I was looking for you was to see if you wanted to—" he shrugged "—do something."

"Something?" she heard herself echo stupidly. She was not putting on a very convincing performance of a wealthy woman who was in control and in charge.

"Lunch? Dinner? I won't offer another tour." His grin was lopsided. "Maybe a tour of housekeeping?" A touch of curiosity touched his eyes.

So he wasn't going to let that go. He'd heard it, and filed it away until now. She thought of going into a silly explanation about how she had a phobia about germs and wanted to see how they disinfected their laundry, or that she was very particular about her pillows and was going to find the perfect pillow. Instead, she tried to stay as close to the truth as possible. "I have this thing about how people do their jobs. You know," she tossed out, "how does a housekeeper take care of a huge staff, get everything done, and nine times out of ten, the guests don't even know she exists?"

He considered that. "Good question."

"I mean, people work all around us, and we can

seldom point out who does what." She warmed up to something she'd actually thought about going from job to job. "Invisible people. People who are faceless and nameless, but if they weren't there, we'd be lost."

He was all serious now, as if he were really thinking about what she said. That took her aback. She'd expected a flip "Yeah, good questions, now let's go somewhere." Instead, he asked a question that rocked her back on her heels. "Can I ask you where your money comes from?"

She didn't know how to respond, so she went for the obvious. "Excuse me?" she asked, with just a touch of what she hoped was haughty annoyance.

He met her gaze. "Listen, I don't care where people get what they have, but from what you've said, you sound like one of those wealthy people who go through a guilt period for what you have and feel you need to improve the lot of people less fortunate than you."

She thought she'd been making it up as she went along, but he'd latched on to the truth in it. When she went to her jobs, she always had an uneasiness with the whole setup of servant and guest. She'd played the games. She had to, but as he spoke those words, she realized that she possibly was a touch militant about it.

She shrugged and passed his comment off with what she hoped was bored disinterest. "I don't go in for guilt," she said. "And I don't want to go into deep philosophical discussions right after a wonderful massage. Let me get dressed and maybe my mind will function better."

"Sure, as I said, I'll wait."

She went in and dressed quickly in her designer jeans, a loose-knit white pullover and low-heeled boots. She didn't question whether she should go to lunch or wherever with Jack; she just thought about what she might be able to accomplish when she did. And she *was* hungry. She'd ordered breakfast from room service that morning, but never ate it. A young woman of about eighteen or nineteen had brought it up for her. She had introduced herself as Sonya and she'd talked nonstop as she set out the food. All Jillian had to do was ask a question and the girl was off and running.

"Is Mr. Prescott downstairs?" she'd asked.

From that simple question, Sonya had let her know that Jack was leaving for an extended stay somewhere, but no one knew where. Jack had been in an accident, but "miraculously" wasn't hurt. Jack was probably going to be scarce in the time leading up to his departure. Jack would probably be in meetings for the day, because some bigwig attorney was at The Inn, and he was Jack's personal guest, staying in one of those fancy cottages that the guy from Las Vegas had been in before.

By the time Sonya had left and Jillian had dressed, she'd left her breakfast untouched so she could get downstairs to make her appointment times at the spa. Sonya had been right about a few things—Jack's leaving, Jack's accident—but Jillian was curious about the attorney. This was her chance to see what direction he was taking on the land sale. Something might slip that would help Ray prepare his offer, something that might assure that the transaction would actually take place.

With just a touch of lipstick and her hair pulled straight back in a ponytail, she braced herself, then stepped out of the dressing room to find that Jack had indeed waited. In fact, he was just about where he'd been when she'd gone inside. His smile came, and she found that she could return it quite easily. "Great. A woman who doesn't dawdle," he murmured. "Now, lunch, maybe a movie, or…?" He actually made a crossing motion on his heart. "I promise no crazy tours this time."

"I think it's well past lunch."

The smile turned into that boyish grin that made her breath catch in her chest. "Oh, I'm sure it's lunchtime somewhere in the world."

"And I'm sure you're right," she said.

"So?" He raised one eyebrow in query.

"So?" she repeated, elongating the single word.

"What's your pleasure? Lunch, dinner, or even breakfast?" Right then her stomach growled and Jack chuckled. "Starved, aren't you?"

She pressed a hand to her middle. "I'm very hungry," she said. "Let's see what they have at the Eagle's Nest."

He shook his head. "It's getting busy this time of day, and there'll be a lot of drinking going on."

He knew his own place, and she could imagine the restaurant the way he described it. "Then what?"

His smile was gone. "Let me pick out a place. I owe

you something spectacular after the way things turned out the last time I took you anywhere."

"You don't owe me anything. You were in that car, too."

"And I was driving," he said. "Let me make that up to you."

"Okay," she said, relenting. She wouldn't fight about this. "Where are we going to go?"

"It's a surprise," he said. "An adventure in dining."

Ten minutes later they were by the side door, and Jack was on a house phone with Malone. "Bring down my leather jacket." He put a hand over the receiver and asked Jillian, "What coat do you want him to get from your suite?"

She didn't want anyone going through her things. She didn't think she'd left anything out, but if she slipped up, things could get messy. "I'll go and get a coat," she said, and would have retraced their path back to the north wing, but Jack stopped her.

"Wait," he said, then spoke into the phone. "Ask Anita to find a jacket for Ms. O'Shay." He met Jillian's gaze again. "What size?"

She told him, and he repeated it into the receiver, then said, "And have my car brought around to the side entrance."

She stepped in, going closer and touching his arm. "Not that red car of yours," she said, cutting into his conversation.

"Just a minute," he said into the phone, then spoke to Jillian. "We're going into town, not into the high country."

"We can take my car. It's an SUV and it's…" She bit her lip. "It's better."

"And who drives?" he asked, keeping the man on the other end of the phone waiting.

"I'll drive," she said.

"We'll toss a coin," he said, then spoke back into the phone. "Have them bring Ms. O'Shay's car around for us."

He hung up and said, "Malone will be here in two minutes."

Jillian didn't know what she'd expected from Malone, but it was two minutes later and he was coming toward them from the other part of the lodge, Jack's leather jacket in one hand and a pale suede coat with a faux fur collar in the other.

"Here you go, boss," he said as he gave the jacket to Jack, then held out the other coat to Jillian. "I hope this is suitable. Anita thought you might like it."

It was like the sunglasses. They had everything a guest could want or need. She took the jacket, caught a glimpse of the label and almost choked. It was very suitable and very expensive and when she put it on, she liked it very much. "It's fine." A staggering understatement.

"Good," he said, then left them.

Jack and Jillian went outside into the coldness of the early evening. "He's good," Jillian said as she looked up at the sky. It was almost brittle in its clarity, and a sliver of a moon hung over the distant mountain. The latest snow had been little more than a dusting of white. "Is there anything your Malone can't do?"

Jack tugged at the cuffs of his jacket. "I haven't found anything yet."

The sound of an engine came closer, and she looked over to see her SUV pulling up. When the car stopped, she hurried around to the driver's side, and when the valet got out, she got in behind the wheel and closed the door. She glanced at Jack, who hadn't moved, then he opened the passenger door and looked in at her. "Are you serious?"

"Are you one of those men who can't stand to let a woman drive?"

He got in, and as he sat back, he cast her a direct look. "Okay, you drive, but I give directions."

She put the car in gear. "You don't know me if you think you can give me directions."

Chapter Eight

Jack didn't take his eyes off Jillian as she drove the SUV toward the entry. He just *bet* she didn't take orders. He found himself smiling at the idea that he'd even want a woman who was subservient and dependent. The next thought he had sobered him. He didn't want just any woman. He wanted her. But he barely knew her. They'd gone through a lot together in a short time, but having a need for her, that seemed too much, too fast.

He made himself sit back and look away from her. He made himself flex his hands and press them to his thighs, and he made himself speak about inconsequential things. He almost jumped when she spoke after they turned onto the highway to head south toward Silver Creek. "So, where do you take women when you want to do something spectacular for them?"

He couldn't honestly remember the last time he'd even thought about impressing a woman. "I've got a few things in mind, but spectacular is difficult in Silver Creek."

"Then how about nice, or just good food and forget

about spectacular tonight?" She tossed him a flash of a smile before looking back at the road. "You brought up spectacular, I didn't."

He sure had. "Tell you what, I'll try for spectacular, but if I get stuck on simply great, you'll have to cut me some slack."

"Deal," she said, then slowed.

They were getting close to town, hitting some of the traffic from the public ski lift area. He looked ahead of them and tried to see the town through a stranger's eyes. Upscale shops, trinket palaces that sold every form of souvenir, coffee bars, ski equipment stores and restaurants that had everything from high-end French cuisine to specialty cinnamon buns. Then they eased into the older section, the part of the town that had been standing when Jack grew up, the Silver Creek he'd known back then.

"Just tell me where we're going," Jillian said, slowing even more as the traffic congested.

He saw a man on the sidewalk, knew he was drunk, but barely had time to realize he was the owner of the local bar, a guy they'd always called Pudge. Suddenly, Pudge turned and lurched into the street, right into their path. Jillian must have seen him at the same time he had, because she was already braking and had her hand on the horn. She stopped within inches of hitting him.

Pudge turned, and despite his name, he was almost skeletonishly thin, even in his heavy plaid jacket and big boots. He glared into the car, screamed something Jack didn't understand, at the same time lifting his foot to kick at the SUV's front grill. The impact shook the car, and Jack pulled the door open, yelling, "Pudge, knock it off!"

At the sound of his name, Pudge stopped midway into his third kick, and turned alcohol-blurred eyes to Jack. "Whash…whash…you…you…Jacko, Jacko…"

"Hey, Pudge, you've got to stop this," Jack said as he moved toward him, more than aware of the line of cars behind the SUV. "You're drunk."

"Yeah," Pudge said with a loose grin. "Sure am. Sure am."

"Hey, get out of the way!" a voice yelled, then a horn blared and kept up an ear-piercing blast of sound.

Jack caught Pudge's arm, and the drunken man didn't fight him. He staggered away from the SUV, but Jack didn't miss the way he looked back at Jillian behind the wheel and made a sloppy wave in her direction. Jack got him between two parked cars, pulled him up onto the wooden walkway and Pudge reached to embrace a pillar in front of a small coffee shop.

"Jacko, Jacko, Jacko," he mumbled thickly.

Jack saw Jillian point ahead to an empty parking slot farther down. He nodded, and as she headed for it, he turned back to Pudge, thankful the noise of horns had stopped. "What's wrong, Pudge?"

"It's Williamette, man. She's hard. Real hard."

"She kicked you out again?" Jack had heard from someone that Pudge and his fourth wife had been having troubles.

"Yeah, she did." He hugged the support and closed

his eyes. "She's…she's a good woman, but I can't…" He licked his lips. "Wash the difference? Don't matter." He was mumbling now, and Jack could tell he was on the verge of passing out. "Just don't matter mush…mush…"

"Is he all right?" Jillian asked as she approached them.

Pudge opened his bloodshot eyes and saw her as she came to Jack's side. The man puckered his lips and tried to whistle, but he didn't get more than a puff of air. "My…my…my," he said. "Ain't she…beuff…" He tried again. "Beuffal." That was the closest he was going to get to "beautiful."

"He's drunk."

As Jack said, "Good observation," Pudge said, "Damn right" as clear as anything.

"I could have killed him," she said.

"You didn't. You're a great driver. No damage."

"Oh, Williamette, she ain't gonna let me off," he muttered.

Jillian looked at Jack. "Williamette?"

"Pudge's wife. Number four."

"Yeah, four," Pudge said thickly, and held up three fingers.

"We need to get him someplace safe," Jillian said, but that project was taken out of their hands when Charley came up behind them.

"I got a call that some drunk was almost killed." He nodded to Jillian. "Sorry you're having such a hard time with this town and cars." He went closer to Pudge, caught his hand in his, then pulled Pudge's arm over his shoulder and supported him. He looked at Jack. "I'll get him to the jail and let him sleep it off before William-ette sees him."

"Bless you, Charley," Pudge murmured as the sheriff adjusted his hold on him.

"Need help?" Jack asked Charley.

"I got it. Todd's coming to give me a hand."

"Thanks." Jack watched Charley start down the walkway, then his deputy, Todd, was there, and with a sober man on each side, Pudge was on his way to jail.

Jack turned to Jillian, who was watching the three men move off down the street. "Sorry about that," he said. "I promised no cliffs, no bluffs and no deers. I wasn't thinking about any drunks. I promised spectac-ular and this happens."

"I'm just thankful that he didn't get hurt," she said, her eyes narrowing as the men got farther and farther away.

She sounded sincere, and it surprised him to realize that any other woman he might have been going to dinner with would have been at the least, annoyed, and at the most, furious that a man like Pudge had inter-rupted their plans. But Jillian had sounded concerned, and she'd acted kindly. The more he was around her, the more he knew that she was not a lot like anyone he'd known in his life. And he'd known a lot of people.

He thought of something then and touched her arm. When she turned to him, he said, "I promised you spec-tacular, and I meant it. You deserve it."

She frowned at him. "You don't have to—"

"Yes, I do." He slipped an arm around her and, with her close to his side, they walked in the direction Charley and Todd had taken Pudge. A few people recognized him, nodded, said, "Hello," and he kept going with Jillian. He got to her car, then let go of her and held out his hand. "I'll drive."

She didn't argue, but just dropped the keys in his hand. "Okay."

"That was easy," he said as he gripped the keys.

"Yeah, it was," she said, and got in on the passenger's side.

Jack climbed behind the wheel and within a few minutes he'd merged into the traffic on the main street and had barely gone a block before he cut left into a delivery alley by Rusty's Diner. Jillian sat forward and peered out at the wood-fronted building, then glanced at him. "This is spectacular?"

He shook his head. "It's good, but it doesn't come up to spectacular. Wait right here. I'll be back in a minute."

He got out and headed into the diner. In five minutes, he returned with a basket he'd had the waitress prepare, put it on the rear seat, then got back into the car. "Here we go," he said, casting Jillian a quick glance before he reversed out onto the main street and headed south.

"What are you up to?" Jillian asked.

He was enjoying this. It wasn't something he'd thought of doing before, but now it seemed like a terrific idea, and he felt as excited as a schoolboy. "You'll see. I'm a man of my word."

They passed the last houses of the town, then were on the winding road that headed south, and if you went far enough, it took you to Las Vegas. He wasn't going there.

"Won't you tell me where we're going?" Jillian asked.

"You *are* curious, aren't you?"

"I told you I've been known to be *too* curious."

He spotted what he was looking for and turned left off the highway onto a driveway that he hadn't used for five, maybe six years. Security lights were on at the gates that blocked their way. The place was well taken care of, even if no one lived here. The hired maintenance men did a good job. The snow was cleared, and when he put in the code at the security box to open the gates, the barriers swung back immediately.

When they drove through onto the property, Jillian leaned forward again, much the way she had at the diner. He knew she saw what he saw, the two-story house with lights on that would suggest someone was there. No one was. The circular drive gave access to the massive portico that protected the entry from the snow. He turned off the main drive, cut to the right onto a secondary drive that was free of snow, too—a route that led to a building that, at one time, had been a stable. There hadn't been a horse there for at least ten years.

The stone walls of the stable were cast in a hazy glow from lights inset in the eaves. He pulled to the end of the building, then stopped and turned to Jillian. She wasn't looking out at the surroundings, but at him. "What is this place?" she asked.

He took in her shadow-softened features. "It's where I lived for a while. My parents' house. No one lives here, now."

She didn't move. "Why are we here?"

"To give you spectacular. It's just about the most spectacular thing to be had in Silver Creek."

She looked puzzled. "Here?"

He motioned to the stables. "In there."

She didn't question him, and he was thankful she didn't. He didn't have a lot of answers right then. But he knew that he wanted to show her something.

"Stay here until I come back to get you," he said, then got out, leaving the car running. He picked up the basket from the back, then headed toward the stables. The maintenance crew had been busy here, clearing the snow from the pathways and even from the outside stairs that went up to the stable's upper level. He climbed the stairs, put in the code on a pad by the door, then with a look back at the car and Jillian waiting in the warmth, he stepped into the only place on the estate that he'd ever liked.

Jillian watched Jack disappear into darkness, and for a moment she felt a bit panicky being all alone. She didn't take her eyes off the stables, then she saw a light in a window in the upper story. It flickered, then grew, and she realized Jack must have lit a fire. Another light came to life, four windows down, and for a split second she spotted Jack, then he disappeared again.

Nothing had gone the way she'd thought it would this evening. Have dinner with Jack. Find out about the attorney he'd brought to The Inn. Simple. Get facts. Now she was at some dark estate where his family didn't live, and he had promised her spectacular. Just when she'd decided to get out and go after him, Jack emerged from the stable and headed for the car. He opened her door. "Turn off the engine, but leave the keys and come on inside."

She killed the engine, got out and went with Jack to the steps, then stopped. "I have a confession to make," she said, and the cold was starting to cut through her expensive designer jacket. "If this is to do with horses, I appreciate the thought, but I'm scared to death of them."

He shook his head. "No horses."

"Okay, I trust you," she said, simple words, but she meant them.

"Let's get inside before we freeze," he said, and took her hand as if it were the most natural thing in the world.

They went up the stairs together to the second level, then Jack led the way, never letting go of her hand, into a wide hallway lit by two carriage lamps. The scent of wood smoke and old leather hung in the air. Four doors off the hallway were closed, but the one at the end was open.

Jack took her toward it, then let go of her hand and stood back to let her go in first. She saw the flickering light of a fire, then took a step into warmer air. The fireplace on the far wall gave off the only light in the space, but Jillian didn't look at her surroundings right then.

All she saw was a wall of glass at the back, maybe twenty feet across and ten feet high. Through the glass, she saw the world. She went closer, stunned at the sight. They were in the mountains, closed in on all sides, but in this place, the mountains fell away and she could see forever. She felt Jack behind her, then his hands on her shoulders.

"It's the only place you can see this. It goes for miles and miles, and see that glow way off in the distance?"

She saw it, the light faint and arching into the darkness looking for all the world like the sun coming up on the horizon. But it was night and the sky was dark, and the glow didn't stop the darkness. "Yes."

"I think that's Las Vegas," he said, "although people have told me there's no way it could be."

She'd been stunned by the view of Silver Creek when Jack had taken her to the mountain, but now she felt as if the world was at her feet. "It's...it's..." She couldn't find a suitable word, but he did.

"Spectacular," he whispered.

"Oh, yes," she breathed.

He let her go, and when she turned, she saw him with the box from the diner, and he was setting out what looked like a picnic on a low table behind them. A couch was turned to face the view, and two chairs made a semicircle. And she saw something else. She went to one side of the fireplace and knew that it was what she'd thought it was: a partially destroyed wine barrel.

One side was broken, missing pieces of wood. The

central metal strap that retained the slats was broken, but the top and bottom metal was in place. "This can't be the barrel, can it?"

"That's it, in all its glory. A reminder." She turned, and Jack motioned her to him. "It's ready. I promised you dinner and here it is."

She went over to the couch, and when Jack sat down, she followed suit. "I forgot to be hungry," she said, and looked down at what looked like simple sandwiches, potato chips and a bottle of... She leaned closer to see the label. "House red?"

"That's the only wine Rusty had," he said. "I was pushing for champagne, but that would have meant going back to find it."

"This is perfect," she said, and meant it.

The air was getting warmer all the time, and when Jack took off his jacket, she took off her coat. He laid them on a table to one side, then poured wine for both of them. They ate in silence, the sandwiches passable, but it didn't matter, not with that view. Finally, Jack sat back and cradled his glass of wine. "I'm going to miss this place."

Jillian sipped more wine and curled up against the arm of the couch, tucking her feet under her. She rested her wineglass on her thigh and looked at Jack. "Then why leave?"

"Why not?" he responded before he drained his wine and sat forward to pour some more for himself.

The people Ray represented would kill to have this

property, she thought. The other property would be forgotten the moment they saw this place. They'd expand the access to the view here and build on it. "So, your parents are gone, and you'll leave, and this place will…what?"

"Be here. Sit empty, unless my parents decide to come back, which they won't."

"If they don't want to be here and you don't want to be here, why not just sell it?"

"Good question," he murmured, stretching out his legs and letting his head rest on the couch back.

"Why don't you use this as an auxiliary location for The Inn?"

"I don't want to expand. I'm trying to simplify my life." He drank more of his wine, then looked at her. "I don't want to talk about business, or expanding, or my parents."

The flickering light from the fire cast his eyes and jaw in shadow. "Then what do you want to talk about?" she asked.

"How about we talk about you? About why you came to The Inn? About why you're here alone?"

She'd asked for that. She'd opened the door. "I came to get away, and I'm here alone because I'm here alone."

He snorted and reached for the wine bottle to top off his glass. "Now, that's a non-answer." He sat back.

"I don't like talking about myself." That was true.

"Well, we're narrowing down the field of acceptable conversation quickly, aren't we?"

"Okay, how about Mr. Daniels? What happened to him?"

"He's in rehab near Las Vegas," he said.

"How about your other guests? Anyone interesting?"

He studied her for a long, uncomfortable moment, then shrugged and drank more of his wine. "Moderately interesting."

She was trying to get around to asking about the attorney, but he wasn't giving her any opening. She made a stab at making her own opening. "You know, I shouldn't have been driving at all when we met up with Pudge."

That got his attention. "What?"

She drank more of the wine and felt the mellowness of it start to seep into her. "I didn't have a driver's license with me. It's at The Inn. I didn't even bring my purse."

"When did this truth come to mind?" he asked.

She never looked at him. "Oh, about the time you stopped Pudge from kicking my car. There he was and I was thinking that I didn't even have my driver's license with me." She braced herself, then turned to him. "Do you know a good attorney just in case I get in trouble over it?"

He chuckled. "I won't tell, and if you don't tell, you won't need an attorney."

Damn it, he hadn't taken the bait. "Good point. Pudge won't remember enough to even ask if I had a license."

"He won't remember much of anything," Jack said, and drained the last of his wine.

"Tell me something, how in the heck did a man like Pudge, who is as skinny as a rail, get that name?"

"Josh told me once that Pudge had been pretty hefty as a little kid, got the nickname, and it stuck, even when he got thin and tall."

"Did you have a nickname?"

"Me? Yeah, more than one, but none of them stuck. How about you?"

That tightened her chest. "My dad used to call me Rosie. He did until I finally asked him not to do it anymore."

"And did he stop?"

She remembered when her dad had stopped calling her that. She felt her eyes smart and blinked quickly before she sat forward and poured herself more wine. She didn't speak again until she had another swallow and sat back against the arm of the couch again. "He doesn't call me that anymore."

She hadn't thought about this for ages. Rosie. She'd give anything if he'd call her that again. She drank more of the wine, but for some reason, her hand was unsteady and wine splashed onto her jeans. "Oh, shoot," she said, and took a napkin that Jack offered her. She pressed it to the denim and muttered, "Great, just great."

She went to put her glass down and didn't realize how unsteady she was until Jack covered her hand with his and took the glass out of her grip. He put it down, but didn't let go of her hand. "Jillian, what's wrong?"

She shrugged, pulling away from him. "I'm just clumsy, that's all." She wrapped her arms around herself and pressed into the curve of the couch. "I've always been clumsy."

"I didn't mean spilling the wine. You're shaking."

She wanted to say she wasn't, that he was imagining things, but he wasn't and she couldn't stop shaking. She looked at her wineglass on the table. She wanted another drink, but she didn't want a repeat of what had just happened. "And I am a klutz."

Jack shifted, reached for her glass and offered it to her. "Fair enough," he murmured. "More wine?"

She couldn't believe what an exercise in frustration just getting a simple drink of wine had become. She put out her hand, quickly took the wine from Jack and got it back to her lap with both hands wrapped around it, without mishap. "Thanks," she said. She lifted the glass to her lips and if Jack noticed the shaking was still there, he didn't comment on it. She took a drink, then another before returning the glass to her lap.

As the heat spread in her middle, Jack said, "Mule."

She blinked at him. "Pardon me?"

"My nickname."

She'd forgotten they'd been talking about nicknames. "Mule? Why would they call you that?"

"The wine barrel incident," he said, then frowned. "As in being stubborn as a mule. As in never giving up." He took a drink, then finished with, "I just never give up. How about you?"

She didn't give up. She couldn't. "No, I don't. But it's not being stubborn. There are just times when you can't." She drank more wine, and found herself saying something that she hadn't even allowed to solidify in her mind until that moment. But it explained the last ten years for her. "There is no way I can give up when I'm the only one who can do what needs to be done." She glanced away from Jack and to the scene through the windows. "When you hold up the world, you can't shrug." That sounded overly dramatic and she felt vaguely embarrassed at having uttered it. But that was the way she'd felt for years. And so weary. She looked down into her wine. "You just can't shrug."

"What world do you have to hold up, Jillian?"

Maybe it was the wine or the gentleness in his question, or her just being so incredibly tired of it all, but words spilled from her. "When I was in my first year of college, my mother died. I never expected…" She drank more wine, then regripped the glass in her lap. "She was gone, and the world got shaky. My dad took it really hard. I'd never seen him as anything but bigger than life. Johnny O'Shay. He made things happen. He was the one who was strong and could do anything." She glanced at the wine bottle and without her asking, Jack reached for it and tipped more wine into her glass.

She took another drink. "But gradually he changed, and when I'd go home for summer break or the holidays, he just retreated."

"People deal with grief in different ways," Jack said.

"I know. But this was more than just grief. Maybe my mother held up *his* world before she died." Jillian sipped some more wine and waited for the heat to warm the chill in her middle. It didn't touch it. "I don't know. I just know that Dad gradually disappeared. Johnny O'Shay was still there, but the man he once was, was gone."

She took a deep breath and let it out slowly. Jack didn't say anything, and she heard herself speaking again. "And it was up to me to take over balancing the world, trying to keep some semblance of a normal life." She bit her lip. "That was the hard part, actually," she said, looking at Jack, meeting his dark eyes. "I didn't know what normal should be. So I made it up, and took care of things—and that's what I do." She lifted her glass in a mock salute, surprised that her hand was dead steady right then. "To normal," she said, and drained her wine.

Jack didn't join her in the toast. He didn't move. She didn't know how much wine she'd drunk, but it hadn't been enough. She could still feel the sharp edge in her words, and she could sense the pain that lingered, not quite touching, but always teasing her with its presence. "Sorry," she muttered. "I don't usually do this. I don't get into the 'whys' or 'whats' in life. I just do it."

"And you hold up the world?"

She laughed at that, but even to her own ears, the humor wasn't there. "That was me being a drama queen," she said. "Sorry. It's the Irish in me. That's why my dad called me Rosie, as in 'Wild Irish Rose.'"

She hadn't realized she was shaking again until Jack's hand touched her hands and pried the wineglass from her clenched fingers. He put it to one side, then buried her hands between both of his. He leaned closer. "Don't do this."

Do what? She was boring him, pouring out this nonsense on an innocent bystander. "I'm sorry." The wine was making her mind muzzy, and instead of pulling away from his hands, she found herself lacing her fingers with his and holding on. "It's just been a weird time lately, and I'm tired." That was so true it almost hurt.

"So that's why you're here?" Jack asked. "You're getting away, taking a break?"

She'd thought she was here doing a job. But Jack's words blew that notion away and left another, more basic reality in its place. She was running, getting away, taking any opening she could to leave her life behind. She even playacted at other lives, at being rich and carefree. Making up people, the way she'd made up a new Jillian for Jack. If he hadn't asked, she wouldn't have had to admit that her life was less than real, and she could hate him for doing that to her.

She looked at him and knew that was a lie. She couldn't hate him. If the Jillian she'd been playacting at The Inn and this fake life she'd been living here had been real, she could have let herself feel a lot for Jack Prescott, and hate wasn't part of that. That thought panicked her, and she stood quickly, knowing that she had to get out of there before he touched her again and before she let her crazy thoughts come to life.

Chapter Nine

Jack was taken by surprise when Jillian pushed to her feet—but then slowly sank back onto the couch, leaned forward and buried her face in her hands. She groaned. He watched her, felt the ache in her with each uneven breath she took. He'd never been a knight in shining armor. He'd never wanted to be. When someone got needy, he left. When someone wanted more from him than he wanted to give, he left. But he wasn't leaving Jillian.

He touched her shoulder, then moved toward her and put his arm around her. She didn't respond at first. She just sat there. "Jillian, it's okay," he whispered, and hoped it would be. That he could make it okay.

"Why did you have to touch me?" she said with a heavy sigh.

He could explain, but he had a feeling she didn't want to hear that he couldn't have sat there and not touched her. "Come here," he said, and pulled her into his chest. She stiffened, and he thought she'd push away, but at the last moment, she sank into him, burying her face in his shirt.

Her hands were flat against his chest and then she weakly slapped that chest before saying, "I should hate you."

That was the last thing he'd expected her to say. "Why should you hate me?"

"You…you made me…" She stopped on a shuddering breath. "I don't."

"Thank goodness," he said. He meant it.

"I'm not another Mr. Daniels, am I?"

He smiled at that. "I can guarantee you, you aren't a Mr. Daniels."

"No, I mean, I'm a guest and you're just being…nice."

Nice? He'd seldom been labeled that. "Ah, Jillian, I'm not usually called nice."

She rested against him and he stared out at the view. He'd always looked at it before and thought about the possibilities of having the world at his feet. Now he looked at it and thought about a woman who felt she had that same world on her shoulders. He closed his eyes and slowly rubbed her back.

"Oh, my goodness," she said, and took a shuddering breath.

He eased her back, looked down into her shadow-softened features and knew that whatever he'd expected to happen here didn't come up to the reality. Sitting here with her, feeling more connected to Jillian than he could ever remember being with another person. Feeling a need to protect and heal. It was both incredible to him and, on some level, terrifying. He didn't want it, but he couldn't push it away. He couldn't push *her* away. "So, you don't hate me. We have that settled, yes?"

"Yes," she said, then touched her tongue to her lips.

He had the craziest idea that he would remember the taste of her when he'd kissed her. That it lingered deep inside him. He leaned toward her, touching her mouth with his and the dream memory overlapped with the reality. He pulled her closer and she came to him. Her arms went around his neck, holding on to him, and all he wanted to do was taste more, to feel more, to know more of Jillian.

He took what she offered, losing himself in the sensations, letting his body respond, and he shifted, pulling her onto his lap. Her legs straddled his, and then curved around his hips. Her breasts were against his chest, and he felt every angle and curve of her body where it touched his. Her hands clutched his shirt, tugging at it, pulling it up and away so she could press her hands to his skin.

Her lips left his searching caress to press to a spot near his ear where the scar began. His response to her intensified, and he wanted her more then he could remember ever wanting another woman. He wanted to pull her into him, to be in her, to surround her and have her. He worked his hands under her top, and felt the heat, felt the smoothness of her skin, then went higher and cupped her breast. He heard her gasp, felt her fingers dig into his shoulders. The need was there, a burning, driving need, and it consumed him.

Suddenly he felt dampness on his skin, and realized she was crying. She was holding on to him so tightly it bordered just this side of pain, and there was more than need in her. It was desperation. He shifted, moved his hand up to frame her face, to look at her. The flicker of the fire played across her face, damp from silent tears. She leaned in to kiss him again, and the same desperation was there.

Although it was almost impossible to do, he shut down. He drew back. She seemed to panic and reached to kiss him again, their teeth almost grinding together. But he knew he couldn't do it. He wasn't noble, that was for damn sure, but he knew it wasn't him she wanted. She just needed a body, someone to be there, to let her cry or scream or both.

She must have realized that things had changed. She was the one to pull back now, to look into his face, and her single word cut him to the heart. "Please."

He touched her cheek, then cupped his hand at the nape of her neck. "Come here," he breathed, and gently pulled her into him again. He felt her tremble, and his arms surrounded her. As much as he wanted her, he just held her to him and let his body ease. He leaned back with her, resting against the couch, and she snuggled into him. There was no demand for more from her, no persistent seduction or frenzied kisses. She just rested against him and let him hold her. He realized then how much willpower he'd had not to take her.

At last she twisted away from him and almost fell

into the cushions of the couch. She righted herself, then stood up and fumbled awkwardly with her shirt. She didn't look at him. She crossed to where her coat was, put it on, then started for the door. He got up, grabbed his jacket and ran after her.

By the time he got to the door, she was almost at the bottom of the stairs. He hurried down, and she was already at the car door, yanking open the passenger side. He called, "I'll close up," then ran back up the stairs to do that.

By the time he came back out and went down to get in the car, Jillian was completely still. There were no tears, no signs of any distress. She stared straight ahead, her hands clasped in her lap. He tried to think of what to say, but couldn't, so he started the car and drove back to the gates and off the estate. By the time they got to the entry gates at The Inn, he was starting to think he'd imagined the whole episode at the estate.

They drove up to the lodge, to valet service, got out, and Jack came around to Jillian's side, but she was already heading up the entry steps. He went after her and a thought came to his mind. He'd been following her since she got here. He'd followed her into the party. He'd followed her after the party. He'd followed her to her room. He'd followed her to the spa. He would have laughed at how out of character it was for him to do that with a woman.

Jillian went through the gathering room to the hallway that led to her wing, and he caught up with her at the elevator. She was pushing the call button over and over again and didn't seem to know he was there with her.

"Jillian?"

She stared at the closed elevator door. "What?"

"That's it? You go upstairs and that's it?"

"What more is there?"

He wished he knew. "Nothing, I guess," he said, but he didn't believe that. There was so much more that he couldn't even begin to understand it. But he knew this was over—for now. "Have a good night," he murmured and walked away.

He didn't look back. He went right up to his suite, and Malone was there on the couch reading more files. "Trouble, boss?" he asked as he closed his reading material.

The man was uncanny. "Trouble," he echoed.

Malone frowned. "The land deal?"

"No, it's not business."

"Ah, so it's personal."

He didn't answer as he crossed to the bar and poured himself a stiff drink. He went to the couch opposite Malone and sank into the cushions. He took a large swallow from his glass, then exhaled on a hiss. "How do you deal with women?" he asked the big man.

"I don't," Malone said, and rose to his feet. "I let them do whatever they want to do and get out of the way when they look ready to charge."

Jack laughed ruefully. "Smart man," he muttered.

"A lady's got you in knots?"

That about summed it up. "Yes, in knots."

"What kind of hope is there for a guy like me if you have troubles like that?"

They both laughed, then Jack tossed off the last of his drink and held the empty glass up to Malone. "Hit me, would you?"

"You got it," Malone said, and crossed to pour him another drink.

When he brought it back, Jack drank part of it before putting it on the large leather ottoman. "I'm not available for anyone until I tell you otherwise." He paused for emphasis. "Understood?"

"Absolutely," the big man said, then picked up his reading material and left.

Jack finished off his drink, tried to work at his desk and ended up just staring at the stack of paperwork he needed to clear before leaving. If he'd stuck to his original schedule, he'd be on the road now, probably heading east, maybe going toward Florida with an idea of going to the Caribbean islands for a breather before he started making decisions. But now he was sitting here, wondering when he'd leave and thinking about a woman who drove him crazy.

He recalled her mention of Mr. Daniels, her notion of his being "nice" to guests. Did she think he was just being a nursemaid? That he'd been with her to keep her calm? That made no sense at all. In fact, it made him angry. He'd taken her to a place he never went and shown her something he'd never shown anyone else.

He'd held her and touched her and she thought it was because it was part of his job? Damn! Well, he wasn't going to let that go. He'd find her tomorrow, and even if she walked away, he'd make sure she knew she wasn't just some job, or some nuisance for him.

He'd run after her a number of times, and he'd do it one more time. Then that was that.

JILLIAN AWOKE SLOWLY the next morning, her head fuzzy, but with no headache to speak of. She relived the time at Jack's stable loft from all angles, and every memory came back to the same thing: she'd almost fallen apart, she'd almost let Jack see her real world. When he'd touched her, she hadn't had any sensible thought. She'd just needed more and more. When he'd pulled back, she'd known she'd gone too far. Despite his denial, it had hit her that he was probably doing damage control of some sort.

That's what he did with guests who had problems. He dealt with the problems any way he had to, whether it was by having Malone babysit them, or by listening to her and showing her "spectacular." She hadn't realized how needy she'd been to have someone to talk to about the pressures of her life.

But at some point she'd gone too far and fallen into that "problem" range for him. She'd known it when he'd stopped touching her and kissing her. When he'd looked at her, and she'd almost begged him to want her. When he'd pulled her to him and hadn't wanted any more. She should be relieved that he didn't just sleep with a "problem" to contain it.

Well, she wouldn't be anyone's problem. She didn't want anyone to think she was some rich woman who couldn't handle her life and needed someone to help her. Well, she didn't want to depend on anyone, for whatever reason, to save her. She'd do what she always did, and save herself.

She got out of bed, showered quickly, and dressed in another designer outfit—thin twill corduroy slacks, high-heeled boots and a white silk oversize shirt that she left untucked and falling almost to her thighs. She pulled her hair into a knot at the back of her head and didn't bother with any makeup. She had to make a list of what she still needed to do here and make sure that she took care of everything before she left.

She'd barely booted up her computer on the Queen Anne desk in the sitting area when a knock sounded on the door. She'd left orders for breakfast, and glanced at the clock. They were fifteen minutes early. She crossed to open the door and was taken aback to see Jack.

"Good morning," he said, and didn't wait to be asked in before he went past her.

She hurried after him, getting between him and the computer that was coming to life. As she faced him, she realized that nothing diminished his presence or the impact he had on her. But she steeled herself. "What do you want?" she asked, wishing that the morning light wasn't so clear and that she couldn't see the fine fan of lines at his eyes, or the brackets around his mouth.

"To explain something to you," he said.

She didn't want to go over what happened last night. "There's nothing to explain."

"That's the problem. I think there is." He was in a chambray shirt and jeans, as casual as any man, but the dark eyes were direct and intense. "I'll do this once, then you can do whatever you want with it."

She moved back a half step and the desk pressed her hips. "No, no, don't." She felt behind her and closed the computer cover. "I hate rehashing that sort of stuff. I don't like discussing things to death."

"Then I'll make this simple and only say it once. You are not a problem for me to contain or control. You are not a Mr. Daniels. I took you to the loft because I wanted to do something that you'd remember, and to see it one last time for myself before I left. I was impressed by the way you reacted to Pudge. I feel guilty about the accident we had, and I suspect any time I look over a drop around here, I'll feel more guilt."

She heard what he said, and if it was the truth, in some way it was harder for her to deal with. If she let herself think about why he didn't see her as problem, and why he wanted to do something for her to remember, it all came back to the fact that he thought she was one of his peers. That she was rich and idle and part of his world.

She realized her hands were in fists and she eased them,

pressing them to her thighs. A knock sounded on the door again, but this time a voice called, "Room service."

She got around Jack without making any physical contact, then opened the door. The same girl, Sonya, who had brought her breakfast the day before, pushed the cart into the room. A cheery "Good morning" was tossed over her shoulder as she started to wheel the cart toward the sitting area. That was when she saw Jack and stopped dead. "Oh, Mr. Prescott, sir. Good morning." She darted a look back at Jillian, then quickly backed up and said, "Please, call if there is anything else you need."

The look in the girl's eyes made Jillian's stomach sink. Within minutes the news would be out. The boss is in her suite first thing in the morning, and she could only guess at the embellishments and suppositions Sonya would put with the truth.

She ignored the food. "So, what now?" she asked.

He shrugged, and the movement tested the blue material on his shoulders. "It's your move."

That meant she had no choice. "Thanks for saying that."

"It's the truth. I don't lie. I never have been one to make up lies to make life easier for anyone. The truth is the truth. I was with you because I really like you, Jillian O'Shay, and I wanted to spend time with you."

Every word he said only made things worse. "Tell me something."

"Anything."

"If I were that girl, Sonya, who just left, would you be interested in spending time with me?"

He looked confused. "What?"

"If I wasn't a guest here, would you still be saying what you said?"

"For someone who told me you couldn't think on an empty stomach, you're doing a damn good job of it."

She couldn't just say, "Guess what? The Jillian O'Shay you know doesn't exist." She had no choice on that. She signed a confidentiality agreement with each job she took, assuring the client that no one would ever know she wasn't what she seemed. The client didn't want the competition put on guard, or to remember it somewhere down the line and have it backfire. She couldn't say anything except, "You're right. This all too much before my breakfast."

She waited for him to say something and leave, but he didn't. He came around the cart, effectively eliminating the barrier she needed between them. "I have a meeting with Owen, my attorney, that I can't miss," he said.

That brought the reality into focus. The attorney Sonya had babbled about yesterday was here for business with Jack. "Then you shouldn't miss it," she said. "It must be really important."

"It is. It's about that piece of land. I have an offer that's good, hell, it's better than good, but I'm not sure that letting it go is smart." She wanted him to stop talking, to not tell her anything else, but what she wanted and what she got were two different things. He said, "Then again, if they sweeten the pot…" He shrugged. "That's why I have to see Owen."

"Of course," she said.

"How long are you booked here?"

She had three more days on the job. "Until Saturday."

"I've got an idea. My attorney has a company helicopter he came in on. When he flies out, he's going to Las Vegas. I was thinking we could hitch a ride with him. We could fly there, spend some time having fun, then fly back here, or drive, whichever works."

He made this harder and harder for her. Especially when she saw the start of a smile on his lips, an expression that was filtering into his eyes. If things had been different, she would have loved to take a helicopter flight with Jack Prescott and spend time in Las Vegas without a care in the world. But she had a care, more than one, and she knew that spending more time with Jack wasn't something she could allow herself to do. "Thanks, but I'm going to just take it easy for the rest of my time here."

The smile never quite came to life. Jack nodded, then said, "Sure, okay. I need to get to the meeting." But he didn't leave. He just came closer to her. "But before I leave…" he said softly, then bent down and touched his lips to hers.

The moment he did, any resolve not to respond was swept away by an instant fire. As she was lifted in his arms, her legs wrapping around his hips, the insanity of it all staggered her. She didn't want this. She couldn't have this, but her body refused to listen, especially when she felt Jack's response to her, and when his mouth ravished hers.

His hand cupped her bottom and their kiss exploded into a need in her that was so intense, it hurt. Last night her need had been there, but in a different way. This wasn't any need for comfort or connection. It was raw and basic and, at that moment, unquenchable. She answered him kiss for kiss, and shuddered when his hand slid up her back under her shirt and pulled her tightly against him.

She tasted his skin, buried her face in his neck and felt his heat and strength. She dug her fingers into his hair and felt the scar.

His voice was a low rumble in her ears, a whisper that seemed to be everywhere. "Oh, my God," he groaned.

Her head arched back, and he found her exposed throat with his mouth. She was against a wall, her back braced against coldness, her breasts heated by Jack's body. She frantically tugged at his shirt, pulled the cotton free of his waistband and touched his naked skin. She felt his heart racing against her palm, then she pulled and heard buttons pop before her tongue sought the sleek heat of his chest. Then she pressed her lips to a pulse that beat frantically in his throat.

He twisted with her, and somehow they were at her bed, still mussed from her restless sleep. They fell into it together, and he was over her, but he never let go of her. He pulled at her shirt, tugging it high and exposing her barely covered breasts. His touch last night had sent sensations through her that had stunned her, but now, with him over her, his hand pulling away the fine lace, then finding her nipples, she cried out.

His lips followed his touch, tasting one nipple, tugging at it, and she arched hard against the contact. She heard low groans and knew they had to be coming from her. She knew that her stupidity was only challenged by her need for this man. She'd never wanted anything this way before, or felt so desperate for a completion that was so tantalizingly close.

Jack moved back, off the bed, and she was frantic to have him not leave her. She couldn't take a repeat of last night when he'd stopped everything and just held her. She wanted more than holding, and when she saw him standing over her, his desire straining against the confinement of his jeans, the world stood still. Nothing existed but this moment, here and now. His hand touched the zipper, but stopped when a knock sounded on the door to the suite.

Jack stared down at her, his eyes raking her naked breasts, then met her gaze. Neither one spoke, then a voice cut into the silence. Malone. "Boss? We've got a problem."

When the other man spoke, Jillian felt as if ice water had been thrown over her. She felt the coldness wash around her, and sanity came back with a pained clarity. She was crazy. Jack was her peculiar form of insanity. A simple kiss had driven her over the edge.

Jack leaned over her, pressed his lips to her forehead, then stood back. "Wait," he said, then he turned and strode out of sight.

She didn't wait. She got up, refastened her bra and fixed her shirt as she moved away from the bed to the windows. She stared out at the day and didn't turn until she heard Jack coming back. She hadn't even tried to hear what he and Malone had talked about.

"Sorry," he murmured, flicking his eyes over her before meeting her gaze. "Malone's taking care of the problem."

He didn't say a thing about her being out of bed or her clothes being fixed. He frowned at the buttons gone from his shirt, said, "Damn," then simply tucked in the tails and didn't seem bothered that it wouldn't ever be buttoned again.

He came close to her, and she found herself tensing. His eyes never left hers. "I'm not apologizing for that," he said. "And it wasn't damage control."

She wished it had been, and she should be the one apologizing. "You've got a meeting," she said.

"Sure do." He hesitated. "I'll find you when I'm done."

"No, I need to…" She shrugged. "I need time to myself."

He exhaled with a shake of his head. "I thought we understood each other."

Heaven help her if he really understood her. "We do, and I'm just saying that this can't happen."

"Well, it sure as hell almost did," he bit out.

She flinched and didn't bother to try to hide it. "But it didn't."

He reached for her hand and touched the wedding band. "Is this really your mother's?" he asked, his expression edged with what could have been distaste.

She wanted to say she didn't lie, but she did, all the

time, especially to him. "Yes, it is," she said, and drew her hand back.

"I'm going to fly to Las Vegas with Owen and I'll be back tomorrow evening," he said. Before she knew what he was going to do, he had her by the shoulders. He kissed her quickly and fiercely, then drew back. "Tomorrow," he said, then he was gone.

Jillian stood there for a very long time, her fingers pressed to her lips, trying to let the ache in her body ease. Tomorrow. No, there wouldn't be a tomorrow.

Chapter Ten

Jack met Malone and Owen in his suite. Owen stood as Jack strode in, and before the attorney could say anything, Jack spoke. "We can do this all on the flight, or at your offices when we get to Las Vegas," he said. "I'm ready to leave now."

Owen Grace, a small, dapper man in a steel gray suit, had an impressive dark mustache that contrasted with a full head of almost white hair. He jumped at the chance to get going, but asked, "You're coming with me? I thought you wanted to do it all here."

He *had* wanted that, but when he'd run into the brick wall with Jillian, he'd decided that leaving for a bit would be a good thing. He could take care of the business and see Cain. Maybe get some perspective. "Changed my mind. Let's just go," he said, without further explanation.

"Good, good," Owen said, putting things back in his briefcase and snapping it shut. "I'll get the helicopter ready. Meet you at the pad in ten minutes?"

"You got it," Jack said, and went into the bedroom to grab his overnight bag.

As he put his things in it, he had to block out the images of Jillian that spun in his mind. Hot passion. Desperate need. Then…a closed look. A drawing back. He should have just walked away. He should have said, "Thanks, but no thanks," but he hadn't. He'd told her he'd see her when he got back.

When he returned to the main room, Malone asked, "You're flying back?"

"I don't know. I'll call before I come back." He went into the office, got his paperwork and put it in his overnight bag.

He stopped for a moment and took a deep breath. He needed order and he needed things to make sense. But he was caught in a whirlpool with Jillian, and nothing made sense. No, that wasn't true. His lust made sense. That tightening of his body when she got close. But what bothered him was something beyond that, something more than simple lust.

He knew it couldn't be love. He didn't believe in love, despite Josh and Cain believing in it so completely they'd changed their entire lives for it. He had to think. This trip might give him the chance to do that. Maybe he'd find the word he was searching for. Get past the lust, he told himself, and figure this out.

"Boss?" Malone was in the doorway to his office. "Any special orders while you're gone?"

"Could you make sure that Ms. O'Shay has everything she needs?"

"You got it." Malone hesitated. "Her reservation's up in a few days, I think."

That brought up another idea. "Keep her suite open. Tell Agnes in Reservations to work it out, but I don't want anyone else to have the suite for at least another week. She can juggle or do whatever it takes."

"Done."

Jack headed for the elevator, and Malone was right behind him. He hit the call button, and looked at the big man dressed all in black. "Any words of wisdom? I can see you're dying to say something."

The big man shrugged. "I was just thinking how women can drive us crazy. They have a gift."

Jack smiled. "Yes, they are a gifted species," he admitted.

"Can't live with 'em, and can't kill 'em, huh?"

A joke from Malone? That was startling. Jack laughed. "I don't want to kill them or even live with them. I'd just like to understand them."

The elevator door opened and as he got in, Malone said, "I hate to see a man on an impossible mission." He shook his head. "Real sad, boss, real sad."

Jack laughed again and hit the down button. "I'll call," he said, and the door shut.

JILLIAN TRIED TO WORK, but after a few fruitless hours, gave up. She closed the laptop and rose to her feet, wondering what in the heck she'd been doing here. She certainly hadn't been doing her job—she'd barely covered half of what she needed to to give Ray a full report. No, she'd been falling into a place that wasn't hers to occupy.

She turned to leave, but stopped when she felt a vibration in the air, then a muffled engine sound. She crossed to the windows and looked out as the noise grew and a helicopter came into sight from the north, heading south as it rose into the grayness of the morning sky.

Jack was leaving. She stared at the helicopter, and as it disappeared, so did some of her tension. He was gone until tomorrow evening. She could breathe and work without worrying about running into him. She could finish up here and leave. She didn't have a choice. She grabbed her security card, pushed it into the pocket of her pants, followed it with her camera phone then left her suite.

She had three things she definitely needed to look into today. Housekeeping was one, hidden food service was another—checking on how the deliveries were made and finding out who The Inn's providers were if she could. She also needed to know the layout of the private cabins. That would be the hardest, getting into one of those very secure cabins. She thought she might be able to get Ivy to show her one, and she killed a twinge of guilt at the idea of using the nice woman to aid her in snooping.

She stepped off the elevator onto the lower level, and instead of going into the lodge, she went farther down into the north wing. She'd just do what she had to do. She'd take Ivy up on her offered tour of the facilities, and go from there. It wouldn't hurt Ivy, and it could get her out of here sooner rather than later.

She passed the steps that led down to the closed doors of the spa, and continued until she faced a door marked *Service*. She didn't see a security key pad and hoped the door was unlocked. She got lucky. It swung back silently and she stepped through it and into a different world from the rest of The Inn. The long corridor ahead was devoid of luxury. There were utilitarian white walls, green-tiled floors and fluorescent lighting. She went straight, then down three stairs and turned left. There were no windows in here, and her boots clicked on the hard tiles underfoot. She walked quickly, checking every door as she went, but didn't see any with a label that sounded like housekeeping.

She turned a corner and there it was, a white door with a brass plaque that read simply *Housekeeping*. She turned the nickel-toned handle, and the heavy door swung back to let her step into another stark area. White walls were lined with gray filing cabinets. A desk in the middle of the windowless room held two computers, a stack of files and six telephones sitting in a perfect line along the closest edge.

Before she could do more than take a step forward, a door at the back opened and Ivy was there. The older woman was all in navy except for a crisp white apron.

"Miss O'Shay. I thought you'd forgotten about wanting a tour of our facilities."

"Oh, no." Jillian made herself smile, even though she was cringing inside at her own ability to lie so easily. "Since I don't ski, I have large chunks of time available while I'm here."

"That's a first," Ivy said. "A guest at The Inn who doesn't ski, or at least, one who'll admit to not skiing. They tend to think it's a very glamorous thing to do."

"I don't mind saying I don't ski."

Ivy took the white apron off and laid it on the desk. "You said your father wanted you to know about business basics?"

She'd forgotten about that embellishment until Ivy said it. "Yes, he does." Johnny had always said if she drove a car she'd better be able to change a tire. She figured that this was just an extrapolation of that. If you stayed at a place like this, you should know how to fold a towel.

"Well, he's a very smart man. No matter how much money you have, you have to know how to husband it and do the most with it. This part of the business isn't glamorous, but if you really want to see how things are run, I'd be glad to show you." Ivy led the way out into the corridor, but instead of going back the way Jillian had come in, the woman went in the opposite direction. They went into a secondary corridor, to double stainless-steel doors.

Ivy pushed one back and led Jillian into a huge room with a cavernous ceiling and every manner of service cart, from laundry to room service to supply. They were neatly stored by use, and every one was immaculate. The Inn might appear rustic, but behind the scenes it was state of the art all the way. The spa had been proof of that, and now this. Housekeeping wasn't just a storage area where towels and pillow chocolates were handed out. It was a planned operation down to the last detail. Jillian saw an entire shelf area stocked with gold-foil candy packets tied with shimmering ribbons. She'd had one on her pillow every night since she'd arrived.

"Wow," she said. "This is a massive operation."

The woman reeled off figures, about guest/helper ratios and how their schedules worked to keep every guest happy and satisfied. "It's a twenty-four-hour job," she added.

"You get everything ready here?"

"Yes, we do. Everything."

"Then what?"

"Come. I'll show you." Ivy went through the room toward a series of stainless-steel doors spaced evenly in the back wall, but motioned to a similar set of doors on the opposite wall. "This is our web of delivery, as one of the girls calls it." Each door was a service elevator, starkly visible in this room, but Jillian bet the exits on the other floors were not so easily seen. Ivy went to the first door. It was marked, "NL3A." "This goes to the north wing, level three, section A."

Jillian looked down the wall at the other elevators, then across at the matching set opposite them. "Those?" she asked.

Ivy crossed to the nearest door. It had a security-code pad instead of a call button. She hadn't seen any security measures on the others. "South wing, all levels, and the last three are the central area, one for the entertainment rooms, one for the bar area and one for Reservations. They bring luggage down here and go to their designated area on the other elevators. Mr. Prescott is very big on being invisible, not showing the guest how much work is needed to give them what they demand. And the first rule is, never do anything in front of a guest that isn't for their benefit."

She pointed to the secured elevator. "Where does that go?"

Ivy glanced at it. "Mr. Prescott's level. We have two maids for his area, and a concierge to service his needs." She smiled slightly. "Although, we hardly need to do anything more than clean up there. That man he hired, Malone, he does everything. He's very versatile."

A buzzer sounded, a far cry from the soft chime that signaled an elevator arrival in the rest of The Inn. The light flashed by the secured elevator, then the door opened. Malone was there. He saw Ivy, smiled at her, then saw Jillian. She saw a moment of real surprise on his face, then a smile was there for her, too, but not nearly as easy as the expression Ivy had earned from him. "Hello," he said to both of them. Then to Ivy, "Mr. Prescott is in Las Vegas, so forget about his room for now. I'll notify you when he's back."

"Thanks," she said.

He turned to Jillian. "Are you lost, Miss? I'd be glad to show you back upstairs."

"Oh, no, she's here on a tour," Ivy said.

Malone raised one eyebrow in obvious disbelief. "A tour?"

Ivy laughed as if to say, *A guest gets what a guest wants,* but said, "Miss O'Shay is interested in how we do what we do."

"Oh, she is, is she?" he murmured, and before either woman could say anything else, he stepped back into the elevator he'd arrived in, hit a button inside, then met Jillian's gaze for a long, uncomfortable moment before he turned to Ivy. He had a smile for her. "I'll let you know when the boss is back," he said to her as the door slid shut.

"Nice man, nice man," Ivy said.

"Seems to be," Jillian answered.

Ivy turned to Jillian. "So, what would you like to see next?"

Jillian didn't want to see any more about housekeeping. This was all she needed here, but she should still get a look at how the private cabins were serviced and take a few pictures. "How do you service the private cabins?" she asked.

Ivy pointed back the way they'd come. "That's done out of the next unit. We use electric carts to get there, and each cabin has a back entrance."

There was no offer to show her the setup, so Jillian let it go for now. Something else intrigued her. "You've been with The Inn since the start?"

"Yes, I have. Right from the first day."

"Mr. Prescott hired you?"

"He did all the hiring back then. Now, he's got staff to do it, although, from time to time, he still does interviews."

"Really?"

"Take Mr. Malone, for example. A few months ago, he walked in looking for a job."

Jillian was surprised at that. She'd thought Malone had been here a very long time. "He actually stopped me on my way to talk to a guest and asked where the employee offices were. I took him there, since I was going that way."

"What was he applying for?"

"I don't really know, but I have this friend in the office there and she told me…" Ivy moved a bit closer and lowered her voice, although they were the only ones around. "He didn't have a résumé with him, but he asked to speak to Mr. Prescott. For some reason, Mr. Prescott had a meeting with Malone, and the next thing we all knew, he was on staff and got the title of personal assistant to the boss."

"Maybe he knew him from the past."

Ivy shook her head. "I don't think so. But I've been intrigued and wish I knew what he'd said in that meeting."

A door opened, then there was the sound of footsteps on the tile floor. A second later, a young girl in a maid's uniform came hurrying into the room and straight toward them. She slowed when she saw Jillian, then paused, waiting until Ivy motioned her forward. "What is it, Donna?" Ivy asked.

"Area twenty has a situation that they need help with."

Ivy looked to Jillian. "I'm so sorry, but I have to go. There's a problem with a guest's needs."

"Is there any way I could see inside one of the private cabins?" Jillian asked, knowing she didn't have time to ease into the request. It didn't matter. Ivy shook her head.

"Oh, no, they're all occupied except for the one the boss keeps for special guests. I'm sorry."

She didn't push. "That's okay. No problem. I think I'll go on up to my room and get a few things done."

"If you need anything else, just call me," Ivy said, then went with the girl to an elevator two over from the one Malone had used. Ivy nodded to Jillian as she stepped into the elevator and the door slid shut.

Jillian glanced around, took a couple of pictures with her camera phone then headed back the way they'd come. She'd write it up, cross off a tour of the private cabins, then see about food service. She had intended to go back to her suite, but when she rounded a corner in the hallway, she spotted a door with a label that intrigued her: *Back Hall Service.* She looked up and down the hallway, then pushed open the door.

She went through it and blinked at the daylight streaming in windows that lined one side of a long corridor. They looked out onto cobbled pavement and a cluster of pines. The walls in here were wood from floor to ceiling and the music she was so used to hearing in the main section was piped in here, too. But where was "here"?

She looked around and realized she must be near the restaurant, and went up a series of stairs to the right. The luxury was coming back, and when she turned a corner, she understood. Somehow, she'd arrived in an outside sitting area for the restaurant. She hadn't noticed it when she'd had breakfast there with Jack, but she guessed she'd missed the fact that the Eagle's Nest was more than one level. This section appeared to be lower than the main dining area.

The roof and one side were glass, and the wall the area shared with the main building was dark wood. None of the guests were out here now, but a few busboys were hustling about with spray cleaner and rags, wiping down the tables and chairs. As she walked through, she had glimpses inside, and the space looked like a pub, not a dining area. Dark wood, brass trimmings and men sitting at a high bar nursing drinks.

She approached the French doors that opened out to where she was and stepped in. It was indeed a pub, and she would have gone right back outside, but something caught her eye. The wall of photos to her left. She moved closer.

They looked like blowups of snapshots, probably guests that gave signed photos to be put up, and the one constant was the backdrop of The Inn and the mountains behind it. She flicked her gaze over the photos, read a few names, then stopped when she recognized a group of men. She recognized two men in the four-man picture. All four were in ski clothes, skis planted vertically in the snow behind them, and their arms were linked.

She immediately recognized Jack as one of the two in the middle of the group. A younger Jack by maybe ten years, then Gordie the doctor to Jack's right, another man on Gordie's other side, and the fourth man at Jack's side. All of them were grinning as if they had the world by the tail. She went closer and saw that the photo was signed under each one—Josh, Gordie, Jack, Cain. Then a date that was just over eleven years ago. She glanced back up at Jack's image. He looked young and happy and as if he really fit here. She knew that didn't come from what he had, but from the men he was with. She narrowed her eyes on his image, trying to blur it a bit to take the impact of it away. He had a life—good friends…roots. All that she didn't have. But that didn't help. She turned from it, and when a waiter asked if he could help her, she shook her head and went back outside.

She crossed to the other side of the outdoor seating area, saw more stairs blocked by a black velvet rope, and when she knew that the busboys weren't looking, she stepped over the rope and hurried down them. Now she was in another corridor that curved back toward the main building, and went only twenty feet before the way was blocked by a single wooden door with a plaque that read, *Service Only*.

When she saw a security panel by it, she was about to turn and go back the way she'd come. Then she noticed that the door wasn't quite closed. She put her fingers into the opening and pulled the door back, then found herself looking into a stone-formed corridor with a low arched ceiling and a cool mustiness that wasn't unpleasant. She stepped inside and the door swung shut behind her, stirring the air around her. Lights inset in the stone bathed the corridor in an oddly intimate glow.

She went forward and heard a low growling sound, followed by a hum that seemed to vibrate the air around her. The farther she went, the cooler it got, and a new scent filtered through. When she saw the corridor widen into a large, deep room, with heavy wooden beams inset in the stone ceiling, she knew what it was.

The room contained rack after rack of wine bottles, shelved floor-to-ceiling in rows. She knew The Inn would have a wine cellar, but one this extensive was very costly. Then again, the cost was passed on to the guest, she thought. She glanced at the nearest rack, and read some labels. Impressive. Definitely. Jack thought of everything. He'd put together a perfect facility. Everything, no matter how large or small, was executed flawlessly.

She wended her way across the space, searching for an exit, and was finally met with a heavy wooden door. It had a security panel beside it and was not ajar. She pushed, but the door didn't give, so she went back the way she'd come. She got to the door she'd come in by, pushed on it and found it ungiving, too. She let out a low groan as it dawned on her that the door had closed behind her and could only be opened by inputting a code. Someone must have mistakenly left the door ajar, or maybe left it unsecured because he was coming right back. Whatever, she wasn't going to be able to leave that way.

She went back to the other door and stared at the security pad with its glowing numbers. She was well and truly trapped. Her embarrassment at Malone's finding her talking to Ivy about housekeeping tours was nothing compared to the embarrassment she'd feel when she had to lie her way out of being trapped in a wine cellar off-limits to guests, and whose contents were worth a small fortune.

She turned, knowing she'd have to wait until a guest ordered one of the bottles of wine and the steward came down to get it. Then she spotted a lifeline. A house phone was set in a niche off to one side. She reached for it, then frowned at the lack of any buttons or dial. She put the receiver to her ear and heard a voice say, "Sommelier." Now all she had to do was figure out a good reason for being locked in Jack's wine cellar.

JACK LEFT LAS VEGAS within four hours of arriving, taking Owen's helicopter back to Silver Creek. He'd intended to meet up with Cain after his meeting with Owen, have a drink, talk and maybe figure a few things out, but Cain had been too busy, not with the usual business demands, but with the needs of his wife, Holly, and her daughter, Sierra. Jack had been partly amused and partly annoyed when Cain had told him he was going shopping for children's furniture for Sierra's room at the penthouse on the top level of the Dream Catcher.

Who would have thought that love could change a man so drastically? Jack had seen it in another friend a few months ago—Joshua, the sheriff's son. Love had bound him to a woman he'd arrested for auto theft. When everything settled, she'd been innocent and he'd been in love with her. On the flight back to Silver Creek, Jack thought about these things. How life changed. How his own life was altering before his eyes.

He'd thought that alteration had begun when he'd met a man in town, Duncan Bishop, and heard how he'd walked away from a world he'd known all his life, knowing there was something else out there for him. How Bishop had reinvented his life. How he'd left behind things that most people craved, money and power. But now, Jack knew that the idea of leaving had been there for a long time, had waited to pop into the front of his mind at the right moment. When he'd realized he woke up every day to things that didn't excite him, or even, in some cases, interest him anymore.

He liked making things go and seeing them grow. He liked being in control, and he liked what he'd done so far. But he didn't feel any connection to those things anymore. Leaving had seemed logical. Going until he awoke one morning excited to be where he was right then.

By the time he landed the helicopter and saw Malone waiting at the back door for him, he was anxious to get back. He was anxious to see Jillian. She'd dominated his thoughts the past few hours, and he knew that was the main reason he hadn't stayed in Las Vegas overnight. He wanted to be back here. With her. And that was the first time he could remember wanting to be anywhere enough to cancel plans and do whatever it took to get there. Maybe, that moment when he was excited to wake up was closer than he thought.

And maybe it didn't mean leaving here at all.

"Boss?" Malone said, reaching to take his overnight bag as he stepped into the lower hallway. "Just got your message. Is there some problem that brings you back early, like the land situation?"

Jack hadn't settled a thing about the land, although Owen had tried to pressure him into making a decision. He was dragging his feet and he knew it. He just didn't know why. "I'm still working on the deal, and I needed to get back to talk to someone."

"Miss O'Shay?"

Jack stopped in his tracks. "How did—?"

"I just got a call from Security. It seems Miss O'Shay got herself locked in the wine cellar." He didn't give Jack time for the shock to settle in before he continued. "She's out now, and Security wants to know what to do about her and the incident. I was on my way to take care of it when they gave me your message about being back early. So I came over to get you."

"The wine cellar?" It was on a full security system and only a handful of people had access.

"Yes, boss, she was locked in good and tight."

Jillian was certainly never boring. "I'll take care of this," Jack said as he shrugged out of his jacket and handed it to Malone. He started off at a quick pace to get to the other side of the lodge and the entry to the wine cellar.

"Boss?" Malone was keeping up with him. "Something's come up, and I thought I'd run it past you."

Jack didn't want to hear about business. Not now. "Just take care of it."

"But, boss, I need to fill you in."

"Look, you know I trust you." They were near the Eagle's Nest, at the doors, and as the greeter came toward them with a huge smile on his face, Jack stopped and spoke directly to Malone. "Just take care of it."

Malone hesitated. "If you're sure."

"Absolutely. Do what you think is best."

"Yes, sir," the big man said.

Jack waved away the greeter and strode into the restaurant, took a left-hand turn just past the reception desk and into a private hallway. He passed the doors to the kitchen and the offices, and went into a secondary hallway whereupon he broke into a trot. He took a curve in the corridor, then stopped when he saw the head of Security by the entry to the wine cellar. "This way," the man said, and led Jack into the transition room between the cellar and the warmer area.

It was then Jack saw her. Jillian was standing by the security door, leaning against the stone wall, and when she spotted him, she straightened. He went closer. No makeup. The same outfit he'd seen her in this morning.

Her hair was still pulled back, although wispy curls had managed to escape to brush her cheeks. Her lips were pale and softly parted. She looked mortified for a moment, then found a smile, a soft, slow expression, and Jack knew why he'd come back so soon.

Jillian. It was that simple.

Chapter Eleven

Jillian was humiliated. First she'd had to admit she was where she shouldn't be, and then she'd had to figure out an explanation for how she got in there. She'd tried the "I'm a guest and I was just exploring and got lost" routine with the sommelier, who'd let her out. He'd accepted it, or at least, she thought he had, until he said his interest was the security of the wine. He calmly called Security, then when they'd come, had gone into the cellar to check on the "condition" of his stock.

The security guard had listened to her dumb story about being lost and going in the other door, then getting locked in. He'd frowned, and hadn't made any comment. He'd simply called someone else, explained what had happened, nodded, then told her they would wait. She didn't know what they were waiting for until she saw Jack. All of her humiliation returned as he approached, and she tried to smile.

Yet even as she died a bit at the look in his eyes, a part of her was so very glad to see him again. She tried to push that down and brace herself. He sent the guard away, then came back to her. He was larger than life at that moment, and memories of the early-morning encounter flashed through her. She felt vaguely light-headed.

"So, you got locked in the wine cellar," he murmured. She couldn't make up some lie for him. "Yes, I did." "How?"

He was in the chambray shirt and jeans he'd worn that morning. Not a fancy man at all, despite all his money. But a man whose impact on her quite literally made her have to remember to breathe. "I went in the door. It shut and I was locked in."

He stared at her hard for a moment, then without warning, he grinned at her. The deliciously crooked grin that exposed the dimple and lit up his dark eyes. The tension from the morning might never have happened. She found herself relaxing a bit. "You know," he said, "if you wanted a bottle of good wine, all you had to do was ask."

Was he going to let this pass? "I'll remember that for the next time."

"Oh, is there going to be a next time?"

That brought heat to her cheeks. "Let's hope not."

He studied her for a long moment, and when she was starting to feel uncomfortable, he finally spoke. "Can we just start all over again?"

Start? Where? "Why?" she asked.

He leaned toward her, putting one hand on the wall behind her, and his eyes came level with hers. "Because I want to. Life is too damned short to waste it on doing this."

"Doing what?"

"You and me. You getting offended, me trying to figure it all out. Why can't we just have a drink, talk and see what happens?"

She would have given anything at that moment to start all over with him, to say, "Hi, I'm Jillian and I can't stay here for ten minutes, let alone for a week on the money I make." She wished she could just tell him the truth and let whatever happened, happen. But if she did, her job was as good as gone. And if it was, she'd lose everything, and the care for Johnny would shift to the state. She couldn't do it. But she didn't want to part from Jack this way. She had to part, she knew that, but she didn't want it to end on such a sour note. A drink. She could do that. "Okay, we can have a drink, but I don't want to go away from The Inn."

"Okay, I've got the perfect place to have a drink and talk and see what happens."

"Good." She made to leave, but he didn't follow. He stood back and motioned to the locked door that went into the wine cellar. "We have everything you could want. I'll even let you choose."

"You're kidding. Aren't you?"

He met her gaze. "Does this look like the face of a kidder?"

No, it looked like the face of a man who could turn her knees to jelly just by smiling at her. "Then what?"

He reached past her to push in a security code, and the door clicked. He pulled it open, and his dark eyes met hers. "Come into my wine cellar," he murmured.

Everything in her told her not to go, but she didn't listen. When the door closed behind them, Jack led the way back into the central area. He went to the left, and at the end of the racks, she saw something she'd missed before—a low archway, which they had to duck under to clear. Jillian found herself in what looked like a sitting area, with a couple of carved wooden chairs by a small round table.

A low shelf held a series of wineglasses and other paraphernalia, including a stack of white linen napkins. A single amber globed light was suspended from a chain in the stone ceiling and it cast softness in its path. "This is where the sommelier does his thing. Choosing and considering different wines."

She tried to act as if she wasn't impressed, but she was. He motioned her to one of the chairs at the wooden table. "Take a seat. Name what you'd like. Red, white, sparkling? A blend? We even have some very good brandy down here."

"I'd prefer wine—any kind," she said. "You choose."

"Okay." He headed back to the racks. He studied the bottles, moved along to the end of one row, then withdrew a bottle. He came back to her and showed her the label, obviously expecting her to know what she was looking at, and she did. She knew names and labels, and this was not just any label. It was a very costly label. "You don't have to—"

He ignored her. "It's my favorite red. It's at its peak."

She sank down in the chair and didn't argue. He went

to the shelf and she watched him deftly open the bottle, then pick up two goblets and bring them with the wine to the table. He sat down and poured a deep red wine for both of them. He waited for her to pick up one glass and put it to her lips before he said, "If I did this right, I'd let it 'breathe' for a while, then we'd sniff it and swirl it in the glass, then swirl it in our mouths, then pronounce it great or horrible."

She took a tentative sip. The wine was rich and mellow. It slid down her throat and spread warmth in her middle. Jack took a sip, then said, "Well, thumbs-up or thumbs-down?"

"Definitely thumbs-up." She glanced around them. "This place looks like it's been here forever."

"Not quite, but close," he said, and drew her gaze back to him.

"You didn't build this when you built The Inn?"

"No, it was built around eighteen-eighty or -ninety."

"How could that be?"

He drank more wine and sat forward with his elbows on the tabletop. "I don't know how much you know about the background of Silver Creek, but one of my ancestors literally pitched the first tent during the silver rush. Most everyone else left, but he stayed, and the town grew out of that. He had this land, acres and acres of it, and built a home here." He fingered his goblet. "He amassed so much money, he was just outright pretentious. The house was the biggest in the town for years, and he had this wine cellar built." He grinned that grin again, and its impact on her hadn't diminished. "The thing is, the old coot didn't drink anything but homemade beer, but I guess he thought he'd look classy if he had a dinner party and he took the guests down to his own wine cellar."

She didn't understand. "You mean, you tore down that house to build The Inn?"

"No, it was gone by then. There was a fire when I was around eight years old, and my parents never rebuilt. The estate we were at last night," he said. "That's what they built to take the house's place. They didn't like it much there, either. That's why Switzerland was such a draw for them. They wanted out and they got out."

"But this was part of the original construction?"

"It was, and while the fire destroyed the house, it didn't touch much down here. When I drew up the plans for The Inn, I had them incorporate this in the design, to make it integral to the food-service area. It's reachable from the kitchens and the main restaurant. It was upgraded with electric lights and the security system, but it looks about the same as it always did. The stone that it's cut into provides the perfect air temperature for the wine, and just in case, we have a backup system for climate control."

None of this had been in her folder on Jack. She thought about the picture she'd seen in the hallway. "It must be wonderful to have roots like this, to know you belong here no matter what."

He frowned slightly at her words. "It was a good place to grow up. Where did you grow up?"

"Mostly around L.A., but some in Arizona. I settled in San Francisco about ten years ago, when I started college."

"So that's home?"

That hit her hard. Home? "Sure," she said, but wasn't at all sure she had a home.

"What do you do there?" he asked.

The soft light in the chamber softened his features and shadowed his eyes. "I work." Wrong thing to say, she realized when he lifted one eyebrow questioningly. She finished quickly, "Charities and stuff."

"Charities and stuff," he repeated before he drained the last of his wine. "And your father lived there before he got sick?"

"No, he was in Portland and he moved there when he really couldn't live alone anymore." She drank more of her wine, hoping it would help her relax a bit. But it didn't seem to, and she wasn't going to drink too much. She had to refocus on why she was here, get him to talk about himself, not her. "So, did you decide to sell the land?"

He considered that with narrowed eyes, then shrugged. "Funny. You and Owen both want to know." She must have frowned. "My attorney, the one I flew to Las Vegas with. He's after me to just do it. It's only land, he says, and it's just sitting there. He can't figure out what I need with it if I'm not going to stick around to expand The Inn."

"So it'll just sit there if you don't sell it off?"

His voice was low and he stared into his wine goblet. "I don't know if I can explain this, but I've hit a point in my life where things aren't making perfect sense anymore." He took a swallow of wine, then seemed disinclined to continue speaking.

After a few moments, she leaned toward him and said, "You know, I don't think life ever makes perfect sense. It's unpredictable and things happen that are out of order and crazy, and you can't change it." Meeting Jack this way was out of order and crazy, and she wouldn't change it. She was glad they'd met, even if this was all there was, wine in a cool cellar, talking about the craziness of life. "I thought you were in Las Vegas until tomorrow evening…."

He drank the last of his wine and refilled his goblet, then sat back in his chair. "Yes, that was the plan."

"But you flew back?"

"Yeah, I did. I took Owen's helicopter back here. He'll drive up in a few days to drop off papers and he can fly back in it then."

He talked about using a helicopter as easily as most would talk about taking a car. She was impressed, but she wouldn't show it. Hadn't she made it a point to let him know that she belonged here? That she had money and time to do whatever she wanted to do? It hit her more and more how foolish she'd been. There had to be a way to do this without making believe that she fit in Jack Prescott's world. Jack must have seen something change in her expression, for he leaned forward, his eyes studying her, and said, "What is it?"

"Nothing," she said, piling one more lie on top of all

the other lies. She wanted desperately not to lie to him. To speak the truth and never lie to him again. Although, truth be told, she knew that if she wasn't pretending to be among the rich and self-indulgent, she'd be way out of Jack Prescott's league. She'd probably look like one of those women who used men for what they were or had.

She put down her goblet and pushed herself to her feet. "I need to get going," she said. "I need…" She couldn't think of a lie to finish that sentence. What did she need?

Jack was coming around to stand in front of her, inches from her, and she knew what she needed. Him. She turned away and hurried back through the main cellar area to the doors. She waited for him to get there and put in the code to open the barrier. But when he got there, he stood, unmoving. At last she said, "Don't tell me you can't open the door."

"Oh, I can," he said, but still didn't make a move to do it.

She finally had to turn to him—and that was a big mistake. He was right there, again only inches from her, and the need she felt for him shifted into something even more. She didn't search for a word. She didn't want one to describe what she was feeling right then; if she didn't give it a name, it might not exist.

Then she knew how wrong she was when Jack gently cupped her chin with his fingers. Dead wrong. She felt a hunger in her, one that had begun at the first and only grew each time he touched her. If she gave in to it one more time, that would be the end of everything. She wouldn't be able to stop.

She balled her hands into fists at her sides to make sure she didn't reach out to touch him. She closed her eyes and held her breath. The next thing she knew, his lips found hers, and she froze in place. She couldn't move at all. She let him taste her, felt his tongue caress her lower lip, his breath mingling with hers. Every atom in her ached to let go, to take what he was offering, to live for the moment. And she came so very close.

If Jack hadn't drawn back when he did, all *would* have been lost. But he did draw back. He was withdrawing his touch, and she made herself open her eyes and look up at him. He was frowning at her, his tongue touching his lips for a brief moment. "I thought…" His voice trailed off. "I'm sorry."

"No, don't. It's me." That was a raw truth. "I just can't…I'm the one who's sorry." More sorry than he'll ever know, she thought.

He ran a hand roughly over his face and exhaled a harsh rush of air. "I've decided to stick around awhile longer," he said. "Maybe we can…" He shrugged. "I don't know. Maybe we can spend some time together and figure out if this thing between us could work."

She turned away and spoke over her shoulder. "I'm leaving soon."

"Three more days?"

She waited. This time he put in the code and the door clicked open. She pushed it back for herself and stepped out. She heard Jack following, and the heavy clank as the door shut. She went up the corridor into a receiving area for the restaurant, then out the entry into the hallway. She didn't stop until she was at the elevator. She didn't have to look to know Jack was right by her. She could feel him. She pushed the call button and waited.

When there was a soft chime and the door slid open, she prayed that Jack wouldn't get in with her. For once, her prayers were answered. She stepped in and turned. He was still in the hallway, and he had one hand on the elevator door to keep it from closing. "Dinner?" he asked.

She was beginning to feel a slight fuzziness from the wine, but that didn't take the edge off the tightening in her being when she met his gaze. "I can't."

He shook his head. "Why?"

"I'm tired." Yet another lie. She hated it.

He whispered, "Sleep well," let the door go, and the barrier slid shut.

She exhaled on a shaky sigh and felt her legs go weak. She grabbed the rail on the wall and held on. This was ridiculous. She was attracted to Jack. No, more than that. She would have had dinner with him anywhere, anytime, if she could have done it honestly. That was the key. Honesty. And she made a decision right then.

She'd seen enough. She knew enough. She could give a good report to her client. She could take it in, end this assignment, and she'd honestly tell Ray why. He could do what he wanted to do with the truth. Then she could come back and be just as honest with Jack. Then whatever happened, happened. If it was nothing, so be it. If it could be more, that would be wonderful. But when she came back, she'd be Jillian O'Shay, a single working woman who lived from assignment to assignment, took care of her father and who had always wanted a real home.

Jack might not want that woman. He might want just a passing fling, an affair without strings. She wasn't sure she could do that, but at least she'd know. She got off the elevator feeling as if a huge weight had been lifted from her shoulders. When she got to her room, she put in a call to Ray.

She told him she'd be back tomorrow, that she'd have the report and she had to talk to him personally. She wouldn't just drop the report off at his office. They made arrangements to meet in the early afternoon, then she hung up. Now that she had decided that she was ending this, doing her job, then coming back, she was anxious to get things in place. She called her father and talked to his caregiver, May, and said she'd be in to see her father late in the afternoon tomorrow. By early evening, she could be at the airport and heading back to The Inn on the five-hour drive. She called to get a flight out of Las Vegas, with a return the day after tomorrow. When that was settled, she put the phone back and felt almost giddy with relief.

Then it hit her. She needed to tell Jack she was leaving early, but would be back. She went to the phone again, and called the desk to ask to be connected to his extension. The woman was very polite, as nice as could be, in fact, but it all boiled down to the fact that she couldn't connect anyone to Mr. Prescott's line without previous approval. When she asked Jillian's name, she came back and was "so very sorry," but she wasn't on his list. She could ring her through to his voice mail and she could leave a message. He could return her call if he chose.

She let her do it, but when the beep sounded for her to begin her message, she hung up. She stared at the phone for a long time, then grabbed her key card and left the room.

JACK WENT BACK to his suite and the minute he got inside, he knew what he was going to do. He sorted through papers, made calls and realized that he was going to sell the land. He'd keep The Inn, but everything else was up for grabs. He couldn't believe how dead set he was on getting the land just weeks ago. Now it meant little, if anything, to him. Something to be turned over. He sat back and swiveled to look out the window.

Damn it, he'd come back early from Las Vegas to see Jillian. He'd wanted to spend time with her. No, he wanted more than that, but he wasn't sure how much more. Now she was leaving in two days. He knew that once she left, he'd be gone, too. Nothing else held him here, and she was only temporarily here. He reached for the phone when it rang. It was the switchboard. He listened to the woman tell him that Jillian had been calling, but she wasn't on the list. He gave her orders to put Jillian's name on his private list and call her back for him.

He heard the phone ring over and over again, then finally go to his voice mail. He hung up. She'd been trying to contact him. He got to his feet and headed out to the elevator. Malone stepped out of the car when the door opened. "Boss, I was looking for you. I need to—"

"Gotta go. I'll be back in a bit," he said, and changed places with the big man. The door shut and he rode down to the main level. When the door opened, he had barely stepped out when he looked to his left and saw her. Jillian was coming toward him. God, she was beautiful. The way she moved stirred him, and when she saw him, a smile played around her lips.

He waited for her to reach him before he spoke. "Changed your mind about dinner?

She shook her head, knocking his bearings out from under him again. "No, I wanted to let you know I'm leaving in the morning."

Before he could respond, a guest was there, reaching out to shake Jack's hand, and while he pumped it, he gushed about the skiing at The Inn. The man left, and Jack turned back to Jillian. But before he could ask her anything, a valet was there telling him that Mr. Malone was looking for him. As he told the valet he'd talked to Malone already, Jillian lifted a hand, mouthed, "Goodbye," and she was walking away. He cut off the valet's response by going after her.

He caught up with her at the entrance to the main

gathering area and caught her by her upper arm. She stopped and turned as he let her go. Her blue eyes were wide with surprise that he'd come after her. She'd actually thought he'd just let her walk away? "Why are you leaving early?"

"I need to."

He controlled the urge to touch her and said simply, "Don't go."

She blinked. "I have to."

"Why?"

"I can't explain right now."

He had a sinking feeling that he was watching everything between them dissolve in front of his eyes, and he didn't want that to happen. He surprised himself when he knew he wouldn't let her go. That wasn't an option. He stood his ground. "I need an explanation."

"I can't. I…" She looked around. "I can't talk about this, but—"

He wasn't accepting that. He took her by the arm and didn't stop when he felt her tense. "We *will* talk," he said, and thankfully she went with him without embarrassing both of them by fighting him. He started to the elevator, then remembered that Malone was there. Before he could think of where else they could go to have some privacy, the elevator door opened and his assistant stepped off. His eyes widened when he saw Jack with Jillian, then he stepped aside to let them in the car.

Jack met his gaze and said, "Later," right as the door slid shut.

Jillian pulled away from him in the car, but she didn't say anything until they were in his suite, with all the privacy in the world. She stood in the middle of his living area and wrapped her arms around herself. "Why did you do that?"

He sure wasn't going to explain to her about the panic he'd felt when he thought she was leaving. He couldn't even explain it to himself. "I wanted to talk and there is no way to do any talking downstairs."

"Go ahead and talk," she muttered, and he knew she was verging on angry. He was verging on frustration.

He moved closer to her and as he did, he felt an awareness of her deep in his soul. This wasn't about her leaving. It was about her not being near him. It was about her not being close enough for him to touch her, to inhale her scent, or see the way her hair curled at her temples. It was about the fact he wanted to wake up with her in the morning. It was that simple and that stunning.

"I don't want you to leave," he whispered in a voice tinged with hoarseness.

She stared at him with those incredible blue eyes. "Why?"

The word hung between them and he couldn't form the words to tell her. Instead, he found himself reaching out to her, feeling her heat and softness, then gently pulling her to him. If she had resisted at all, he would have stopped, but she didn't. She eased into him as if each of their bodies were made to match every curve and angle of the other's. He held her, felt her heart hammering against his.

He didn't want her to go because if she stayed, if she was here with him, he knew that he could love her. That shot through him, exploding in him, and everything made sense. God, he could love her. That rocked his world.

He felt her ease back, her hands pressed to his chest, then she was looking up at him with eyes filled with the same disbelief he knew had to be in his. Her lips were parted and when he felt her tremble, he lowered his head and tasted her. He inhaled her heat, and felt as if the world centered and became incredibly clear.

"Stay?" he whispered against her lips. "Stay with me?"

Chapter Twelve

Jillian could have cried. She'd been so close to making it out of The Inn. She had been so close to making her plan work. Going and fixing things, then coming back so she could stand in front of Jack as herself. So close. And now that wouldn't happen. The minute he'd touched her, it was over and done. She didn't fight it. She didn't protest. She let him hold her and she held on to him. She let her face press to his chest and felt his heart beating against her cheek.

She closed her eyes and felt his hands on her back, then his lips at her temple, and she lifted her face to him. When his lips claimed hers, turning back just wasn't an option. She opened her mouth to his invasion, and she let his taste fill her. She pressed closer to him, trying to melt into him. That was all she wanted, to be one with him. To disappear into him and have him surround her. That was all she wanted.

She circled his neck with her arms and felt his chest press against her breasts. She had no doubt that the need in her was in him, too. The desire that was building and taking on a life of its own was matched by his, and she clung to him. His lips pressed kisses to her eyes and her cheeks, then her ear and her lips again. Then he eased her backward, lifting her up a step, until they were in the next room, in his bedroom.

She had an impression of high ceilings and a huge bed, but her whole attention centered on Jack and his touch on her. They were at the bed, falling back into luxurious softness. He was over her, braced by his hands near her shoulders, and she looked up at him. She touched his face, felt the prickle of a new beard and found a pulse that beat wildly near his ear. He moved back, stood and stepped out of his boots, then he pulled off hers, tossing them down by the bed.

He stood over her and she could see how much he wanted her, but he didn't come back to her. He kept his distance. "Tell me now if you can't do this," he said in a low, rough voice. "Just tell me and I'll stop."

She looked up at him and the truth hung between them. "Please, I want you."

He was still for a long moment, then he tugged his shirt off, and his jeans followed. For a moment she had a glimpse of him in white Jockey shorts, then they were gone and he was naked. Her heart hammered in her chest, and her arms reached out to him. He came to her, and she wanted more. So much more. She wanted skin to skin, with nothing between them.

She tried to undo the buttons on her shirt and he had

to help her, but then the cotton was gone, and her bra was unsnapped and tossed in the general direction of her shirt. Jack knelt over her, her legs between his thighs. His dark eyes met hers as his hand found the fastener at the waist of her slacks. She lifted her hips to help him pull both her slacks and panties off her. Then they were both gone, and he was with her, skin to skin, heat to heat, and she knew that she'd waited for this moment all her life.

He trailed his lips along her jawline, down to her throat, then found one of her breasts. Then his lips caught her nipple and sent feelings through her that made her gasp. He laughed a low, rumbling sound, and caught her other breast in his hand. The touch was overwhelming, making her shake and arch, and then he was over her.

She reached down and found him, closing her hand on him, and he shuddered, his head arching back. He gasped, and any restraint either might have had was gone. He came to her, and she lifted her hips to him, opening herself and wanting him in her. She felt his strength against her, and then he entered her, slowly, so slowly, until he filled her.

Jillian cried out when he started to move, and she matched his thrusts, going higher and higher. Her whole body felt as if it was part of him, and that she could do what she'd wanted, just disappear in him. She wrapped her legs around his hips, pulling him deeper with each stroke, and when she thought it was impossible to feel any more than she felt at that moment, she did. She was filled with him, and the culmination went beyond anything that she thought two humans could find.

She cried out and held on to him, wrapping her arms and legs around him, arching up as close as she could, and she thought that she'd never let go. She never wanted him to leave her. He held her, and kissed her, then they rolled to their sides, still together. Finally, he left her, and he pulled her into his arms, against his chest. His skin was slick and hot, and she tasted the saltiness when she kissed him over his heart.

This wasn't how she'd planned it. The timing was all wrong, but she was here with him now, loving him, and she wouldn't change that for all the world. She snuggled into his side, with her arm over his stomach, and closed her eyes. No matter what happened from here on out, she would have had this night with Jack. She'd store it away with her other memories and cherish it. It might be all she had, or it could be a wonderful beginning. She wouldn't know until she left and came back, but she had this. She was in Jack's arms, her body tender from their lovemaking, and she would take that with her forever.

JACK AWOKE SLOWLY, letting the sensations of Jillian against him filter into his being. The room was dark, everything blurred, but the feelings in him were sharp and true. He'd wanted her, and when he'd told her he'd let her go if she didn't want him, he'd meant it. Although he hadn't known how he'd have been able to let her just walk away, he would have.

She felt him stir, then shift, and she curled into him, her cheek on his chest, her hand splayed on his stomach.

Their legs were tangled and he could feel every breath she took, every beat of her heart. She sighed softly, and he closed his eyes. How could he not have realized this from the beginning? How could he not have known that he was falling in love with this woman? As impossible as that was, he knew now it had been inevitable.

He felt her stir, then slowly stroke his chest, and his body responded to the contact. When he'd climaxed, he'd thought he'd had it all, that he'd been sated beyond bearing, but he'd been wrong. As wrong as he'd been when he'd thought they could start over and take it slowly and not let this happen until the time was right. Wrong, wrong, wrong. But now, it was so right. It felt right. It settled his soul.

He felt her shift again, and he pressed his lips to the top of her head. "I thought you were asleep," he breathed into the night around them.

"No."

"Good." His hand brushed her cheek, then stroked her shoulder, every touch cementing his feelings for her. He ran his hand along her side, then moved to cup the fullness of her breast. He felt her nipple harden at his touch, and he heard her sigh softly as he made circles with his fingers on her skin.

He raised himself on his elbow and looked down at her, brushing at her hair, then finding her breast again. "Thank you for staying," he whispered.

She smiled up at him and started to say, "Thank you," but her words broke on a tremor when his hand left her breast and went lower, to her center. He felt her heat and moisture and he pressed against her.

She began to tremble, then she shifted and got on her knees. In moments she was over him, straddling his hips, and with his help, she lowered herself onto him. He loved the feeling of entering her, of her heat surrounding him, then her moving with him. He kissed her breasts over him, and lowered his hands to her hips, pulling her against him so he could go as deeply as possible.

She started to move and he let her control the pace. He lifted his hips to her, and she met him, over and over again. There was nothing easy and tempered about their lovemaking. It was hot and immediate, the sensations were there right away, the fire growing with such speed that when the apex came, his cries mingled with hers.

He watched her, never closing his eyes. Her head lolled back, her eyes closed as she absorbed every shard of feeling, then slowly sank against his chest. And his world settled into a glow of pleasure that invaded every part of his being, every part of his world. And right then, his entire world was in that room with Jillian.

WHEN JILLIAN AWOKE again, she was alone. She was in Jack's bed, in the suite, naked under a thin sheet, and an empty space was beside her. She sat up, grabbing at the sheet to keep her breasts covered, and she called out, "Jack?" Nothing. "Jack?"

When there was no response, she got up and, taking a throw on the end of the bed to wrap around herself, padded barefoot to the main room. Empty. She turned back to the bed and that was when she spotted a note on the other pillow. It had half fallen to one side, almost off the bed. She crossed to it and saw her name on it in blunt writing. She opened it. *Had to take care of things. Be back by noon. Let Malone know where you'll be.* It was signed with a scrawl that, if she squinted just right, probably read "Jack."

Her heart sank. She'd wanted to talk to him, to let him know she'd be back tomorrow, but she couldn't now. She looked at the clock. She had time to make her flight. She'd leave, take care of making this right, then she'd come back to Jack. She dressed quickly, then scrawled a note on the back of the one he'd left for her. *I have to go, but I'll be back tomorrow. I'll call.* She hesitated, then didn't put what she'd almost written, "Love, Jillian." Instead she put, "I'll stay."

She hurried to her suite, had her bags taken down to her car, which was being brought around, and within half an hour, she was on her way out of Silver Creek.

The trip back to San Francisco was a blur, but she got there by two o'clock, in time to make her meeting with Ray. She didn't even bother changing. When she stepped into his marble-floored reception area, his receptionist, Natalie, greeted her with, "Well, Jillian, welcome back, love. Go right in. Ray's expecting you."

Jillian went into Ray's private office at Platinum Group and found him sitting behind the desk, ignoring the No Smoking signs on the wall as he sucked on one of his ever-present cigars. "Ray," she said, crossing to the desk to put her report on it. "It's all there."

The balding man smiled at her. "So, how'd it go?"

"That's what I need to talk to you about," she said, taking the chair opposite him.

"Trouble?" he asked, sitting forward.

"For you? No, no trouble."

He relaxed a shade, but not much. "Then what?"

She laid it out as quickly and as concisely as she could, and ended with, "I did the job, got the information, and I'm done with it."

"And if there are any questions?"

"I don't have any answers," she admitted. "Everything I know is in there. I don't know if he'll sell the land or not. I don't know what he wants." All she knew was what *she* wanted. "I do know that I won't break any confidence, period." She hesitated.

"I can't do any more on this job. I can't help them anymore with the land deal. I'm done."

Ray understood and didn't argue. He sat back, clasping his hands behind his head as he looked up at her through a screen of cigar smoke. "Where are you off to?"

"To see Dad."

"Good luck," he said, then stood, extending his hand to her. "I'll be in touch when you're needed."

"Thanks," she said, and left.

The ride to the home where her father was cared for took a good half hour in the late-afternoon traffic, so by the time she walked into the old Victorian bungalow that had been redone to house five disabled people, her nerves were on edge. She signed in at the front, then went back to the room her father had lived in for the past three years. It was nice, done in yellows and white, with a screened porch directly off it. It was as nice as could be, she thought, but it still held the pungency of the sick. The odor of disinfectant and medication.

She stopped at the open door and looked in. Her father was in his wheelchair, sitting so he could look out onto the porch. He was still a big man, with white hair. The pajamas he wore most days were pale green and baggy. His hands held on to the arms of the chair and his head was down, his chin resting on his chest. His caregiver, May, with her constant smile, was making his bed.

"Oh, Jillian, I'm glad you're back. He's been waiting for you to visit."

Jillian knew that was a lie, but it was one that they played out every time she came here. "How is he?" she asked, going in and moving toward the wheelchair.

"The same. Good days, bad days. Ups and downs." May smiled. "Like most of us." She smoothed the sheets and fluffed the pillows. "He's not sleeping. He's just waiting."

Jillian pulled a chair with her and put it in a position that didn't block the view of the porch, but let her almost face her father. "Dad?" He didn't respond. Then she touched his hand. "Dad, it's me, Jillian."

His eyes fluttered, then he slowly raised his head. He

was over sixty now, and the lines in his face were deeper, but his eyes were just as brilliant a blue as they always had been. Those eyes looked at her, and he smiled. "Hello," he said in a gravelly voice that sounded as if it wasn't used very much.

"I just got back from Nevada and came to see you. There's a lot of snow there, and it's cold. It makes you appreciate the weather here, even with all the fog and gray skies." She leaned a bit closer. "I wanted to wish you a Happy New Year."

His head tilted to one side and he studied her, then frowned. "I was waiting…"

"For what?" she asked, letting a flicker of hope rise in her that he might have actually been waiting for her.

"It's cold," he said, and turned from her.

Jillian never cried about this. She just did what she needed to do. But right then, tears stung her eyes. There were so many things she hadn't told Jack about her life. But when she went back as herself, she would tell him everything—if he wanted to hear it.

JACK GOT BACK to The Inn from town just after noon and went right to a house phone to contact Jillian. He'd awakened that morning facing Jillian in the bed, and that excitement he'd thought he'd never find was there. A day ahead of him with her. Then he'd had to leave, but the excitement had stayed with him. Now her room phone rang, then went to her mailbox, and he hung up. He turned to go up to his suite and find Malone, but the big man was right there. He seemed relieved to see Jack. "Boss, good to see you. I was wondering when you'd get back."

"I just arrived. I'm looking for Ms. O'Shay. I told her to let you know where she was going to be around now."

"I never talked to her," Malone said.

Maybe she was still in his bedroom, waiting, Jack thought, and headed for the elevator. He hit the code and the door opened. When Malone got in with him, he started to object, but the big man stopped him.

"She's not there," he said, hitting the Door Close button.

Jack cast him a sharp look as the car started up. "I thought you said she never spoke to you."

"She didn't."

The elevator stopped and the two men got off. The place was empty. Jack could feel it. He turned to Malone. "Then how did you know she wasn't up here?"

"She left. She checked out."

The excitement was slipping, and anger at Malone was growing. "Damn it, I told you to let them know that I wanted the suite kept."

"It was, but she left. She cleared out everything."

Jack stared at him, the impact of his words as strong as any punch to his middle. "I don't believe it."

Without a word, Malone went past Jack and into the office to the left. He reappeared with a folder in his hand. He crossed and held it out to Jack. "It's true, and I think you need to read this."

Jack stared at the big man. "What is it?"

"Just read it, boss."

Jack took the folder, opened it and first saw the name Jillian O'Shay, then he read further and he felt his whole world shift and tilt precariously. He caught at the words "Jillian O'Shay is an evaluator" and "credit card traced back to the Eastern Realty Corporation, then the Platinum Group." The company his attorney had been dealing with for the land. "Works undercover to evaluate businesses for clients." Usually "for the purpose of undermining competition." Jack moved to the nearest couch and sank onto the leather, unable to stop reading, in much the same way people's eyes are drawn to the scene of a horrible accident.

Malone stood over him. "She's a snoop getting the goods on your operation. That Platinum Group does broker work for a lot of big hitters."

Jack didn't have to be told that those big hitters were usually development companies that specialized in getting into resort communities and undercutting the existing establishments. His stomach knotted so hard he thought he'd be sick. He got to his feet.

"Where in the hell did you get this?"

Malone stood his ground. "I was uneasy about her. She was down in Housekeeping asking questions, and she was all over the place, talking about things that no guest would have any interest in. That camera phone. She always had it with her. I got this friend and he did me a favor. I got the material yesterday." He frowned when Jack just stared at him. "I tried to talk to you, and you said to take care of it."

Jack crushed the folder in his fist. He'd found everything last night, he'd thought, and now it was all being torn away from him. It was very clear and he could see it. The questions she asked. Was he going to sell the land? Taking a damn tour of Housekeeping. Even asking about selling the estate. A spy. An underhanded liar who got close to him to get information. God, he'd fallen for it. He'd gone all the way, up to thinking he was in love. He'd been had before, but never like this, never left feeling as if he'd been destroyed. He'd never let his guard down the way he did with Jillian. Now it was over. It was done. And he had to live with the rubble.

He uttered a rough expletive and threw the folder across the room. Papers went everywhere and he didn't give a damn. He looked at Malone, not knowing if he hated the man or if he owed him more than he could ever imagine. One thing he did know was, he was leaving Silver Creek, and he didn't give a damn who had the land. He didn't give a damn about anything.

JILLIAN THOUGHT she'd sleep at her apartment, get the early flight back to Las Vegas and be in Silver Creek by noon to see Jack. It sounded good. She was relieved and settled about what she'd done. Now she just had to explain it all to Jack and go from there. But she couldn't sleep, and around midnight, she dialed the number for The Inn.

As she asked for Jack's suite, she remembered that

she wasn't on his list, so she was surprised and pleased when the receptionist said, "Oh, yes, Ms. O'Shay, I'll put you right through."

It rang a double ring, then three single rings before it was answered. But it wasn't Jack on the other end. "Mr. Prescott's suite." Malone.

"Mr. Malone, it's Jillian O'Shay. I was wondering if Jack's there?"

She flinched slightly at his abrupt tone. "No, he's not."

There was no politeness in the response. "When will he be back?"

"I wouldn't know."

She was hitting a brick wall and she wasn't one to beat her head against something that ungiving. So she backpedaled and said, "Could you let him know I'll be in around noon tomorrow?"

Without a word, the line went dead. She drew the receiver back and stared at it in confusion. Why was Malone so rude?

Minutes later, she crawled into bed. It didn't matter about Malone. She'd see Jack tomorrow and that was all she had to focus on. That's what she had to make work. If it didn't, it wouldn't be because she hadn't tried.

But by noon the next day, when she drove back through the gates of The Inn in a cheap rental car she was paying for herself, Jillian was almost sick to her stomach with nerves. She'd thought of trying to call again, but hadn't. Now she pulled the car into the side lot by the private entrance, and got out into a gray day where snow was starting to drift down from a leaden sky.

She stepped into the lodge, and would have gone to the elevator to go up to Jack's suite, but a strong hand on her arm stopped her in her tracks. "What are you doing here?" Malone asked her abruptly.

She wanted to ask him who he thought he was, but instead she said, "I told you I was going to be here."

"Well, the boss isn't here."

She pulled her arm out of his hold and moved back half a pace. "Where is he?"

"Don't know," the big man said.

"Then I'll wait for him to get back."

"I don't think so," he said, and reached for her arm again, but she moved quickly out of his reach.

"What's going on?" she asked, feeling particularly unsteady right then.

"Let me explain," Malone said, and motioned her to follow him into a side office. The room was tiny, and obviously used for little more than a storage area. Malone filled the room with his size and his attitude. He pulled something out of his pocket and held it out to her. "The boss has this. All of it. This is just the top page."

She felt the blood drain from her face when she read the first two lines. She didn't bother with the rest. She pushed it back to him. "I need to talk to him, to explain. That's why I'm back here. I left him a note—"

"No," Malone said, taking the paper and pushing it into his back pocket. "The note was torn up, and the bottom line is, he doesn't want to hear anything you've got to say."

She felt a coldness growing in her, but she persisted. "Please, I just need a few minutes. I was doing my job. It was nothing personal. I didn't do anything wrong. And I came back to explain."

He eyed her intently, and she hoped to see some wavering in him. She didn't. "Too late."

She took a shaky breath, then fumbled in her purse and pulled out one of Ray's cards. "He can call this man. He's my go-between. He gets me my assignments. He'll tell Jack that I only did what I was asked to do. My job."

Malone took the card and pushed it in his pocket without looking at it. "I'll show you out."

She had to know one thing. "Is he here in Silver Creek?"

Malone hesitated, then shook his head. "He left."

When he went to take her arm, she didn't try to evade it. Her head suddenly felt light. Jack had left. He was gone. And she knew that he wouldn't be back for a long time, if ever.

She didn't know how she got to the car, but she did. She was behind the wheel, starting the engine, and Malone stood by her door, his eyes never leaving her, his arms crossed on his chest.

She drove away, down the drive, through the gates and toward Silver Creek. When she went through the town, she knew that she'd never be back, either. Whatever hope she'd had was gone, and she really was just left with the memories. Despite what she'd thought when she was with Jack, the memories would never be enough for her. She knew it would be a very long time before she could even sort through them. Maybe she never would.

Chapter Thirteen

Jillian had been home for three days and she'd done little other than take long walks up and down the steep streets near her apartment. It was cloudy and cold in San Francisco, and she trudged along with her chin tucked into the collar of her jacket, not looking at much of anything as she went. She knew the bay was a block away and if she turned, she'd catch glimpses of its choppy, gunmetal-gray surface in openings between the houses. A wind whipped off those waters, making the chill bone-deep, but nothing matched the coldness in her soul.

If she'd had to, she wouldn't have been able to even begin to explain how she felt. She just experienced it and hoped it would at least ease soon. Maybe go away entirely one day. She hoped so. She didn't count on it, but she desperately hoped so. She turned onto her street and started up the incline to the fifth house on the right. Old and four-storied, it was sandwiched between houses that mirrored its age and height. It was painted blue, set among homes painted peach, gray and green.

She climbed the stairs of the full veranda, went in the main door and glanced in her mailbox, inset to the side of the mahogany door. Nothing. She went up to her apartment and walked into dead silence. Nothing stirred. There was nothing *to* stir. She checked the clock as she slipped off her jacket and stepped out of her running shoes. It was almost five. The worst time to drive around the city, but she needed to go and see her father.

When she'd first gotten back to San Francisco, she'd gone to see him. She'd talked and talked, and he'd just sat in his wheelchair, his face passive and almost serene. He hadn't appeared to know what she was saying, but nevertheless, telling him about Jack and what had happened had helped her in some way. She'd talked until she couldn't anymore, and then lapsed into silence. She knew she wouldn't do it again.

She dressed quickly in her jeans, no-name jeans, not designer. Her shirt was cotton, not silk, and her boots were worn and comfortable, not stylish. She was Jillian O'Shay, pure and simple. She didn't bother redoing her hair. It was in a ponytail, but the humidity in the city made ringlets at her cheeks and temples.

She grabbed her shoulder bag and left. She had to walk a block to get to the garage where she kept her car, a small import that had over a hundred thousand miles on it. It took her forty-five minutes to get to her father's home. She parked as close as she could and walked the rest of the way. She went inside, signed in, then stopped.

For a moment she thought she'd gone mad. The name

above hers was a scrawl, but she'd seen that scrawl before. Jack Prescott.

She hurried back to her dad's room. The door was open, as it usually was, but as she approached, she heard a voice and knew that she hadn't been seeing things.

"I met Jillian at a resort I own, The Inn at Silver Creek. That's an old silver mining town in the Sierra Nevada mountains on the Nevada side. Sort of like Tahoe without the overlaying glamour and size. I was born there. Grew up there. I lived there until a few days ago."

Jack. She felt faint, and put a hand on the coldness of the wall for support.

"It was midnight on New Year's Eve," his low, deep voice continued. "Lots of celebrating. Lots of people. But all I saw was her." He chuckled, a rough sound. "Actually, I ran right into her. Then at midnight, I kissed her." His voice was serious now. "Jillian was all I saw for five days. I was ready to leave Silver Creek, to take off in some sort of self-realization thing. But the longer I was around her, the less I wanted to leave. We talked about a lot of things, and about her holding the world on her shoulders. She's doing that, you know. She's trying to keep it balanced. I admired that in her. Here I was trying to figure out where my world was, and she knew. Then it hit me that maybe all I needed to know about who I was and what I wanted was right there in Jillian. At least, until everything fell apart." He sighed. "And it did fall apart."

She closed her eyes, and whatever Jack was saying was lost in a rushing sound in her ears. The world tilted, and she tried to breathe. Why was he here? What was going on? She tried to grab at control, and found a semblance of it. Then the voice came back into focus. "Thank you for listening, sir. I appreciate it. You take care of yourself, now."

She heard footsteps, and opened her eyes. Jack was in front of her, those dark eyes meeting hers, eyes that did not look surprised to see her. "Jillian," he said in a voice so soft she almost thought she'd imagined him uttering her name.

All she could do was stare. His image was painfully clear. The hair wind-mussed, the shadow of a new beard darkening his jaw, the familiar leather coat. His hands were pushed deep in the pockets. "May said you'd be coming by, that you'd promised Johnny you'd be here and you always kept your word."

She found her voice. "What are you doing here?"

"I had things to do."

That made no sense. He had no reason to be here, not with her dad. She blinked at him, her eyes burning with tears that never fell. "What things?"

"We need to talk."

"But my father…?"

"We've talked," he said, as if they'd really had a man-to-man talk. She knew that was impossible. And it hurt her more in that moment than it had for a very long time.

"Sure," she muttered, and found the ability to move.

She moved past Jack in the doorway without brushing against him, but that didn't stop the scent of aftershave and leather from invading her senses. She went directly to her dad, and the chair she always used was in its usual spot.

She sank onto it and touched her dad's hand. It felt cool, and when the contact was made, her dad turned toward her. His blue eyes studied her, his expression impassive as always. He whispered, "Hello," then turned back to the view out the window.

She was overwhelmingly aware of Jack being there, out of her line of vision, but she didn't look away from her dad. "Dad, I talked to Dr. Sloan yesterday, and he thinks that day trips would be good for you again. Get you out of here for a while, maybe once a week." No response. "I'll work it out and let you know when it can happen."

She realized her hands were clenched so tightly in her lap that her nails were digging into her skin. She relaxed her fingers and spread them on her thighs. "We'll take a drive soon and…" Her voice broke. "Soon, Dad, soon."

She stared at her father's profile, but was still totally aware of Jack somewhere behind her. She'd wanted so desperately to talk to him three days ago, but now she couldn't even bear the thought of those dark eyes looking at her with hate and scorn or, at the least, disgust.

She needed air. She needed to get away from here. She got to her feet, pushed the chair back against the wall, then leaned down to kiss her father on his forehead. "I love you, Dad," she whispered, then turned to leave.

Jack wasn't there. He'd left? The sharp sorrow she'd felt for days started to be outweighed by a blessed numbness. He'd left. He was here for whatever reasons, she didn't care, then he left. The only feelings she could find were loneliness and a degree of disappointment that she had never gotten the chance to tell Jack the truth for herself.

She took one last look at her father, leaned down to hug him, then left. The hallway was empty. She had no idea why Jack had even shown up here. Why had he taken the time to find where her father was being cared for? Why would he talk to a man who obviously didn't have any comprehension of the world around him? Why would he tell the man abut meeting her and goodness knew what else?

She went down the stairs, crossed the foyer and stepped out into the chilly evening air. The city was all around her, the sounds peculiar to it filling the air. Then she knew it wasn't over with Jack, after all. He was waiting. He was by the curb, leaning back against the bright red Porsche that hadn't been parked in that spot when she'd arrived. She would have seen it.

He leaned back against the car, his arms crossed on his chest, his eyes on her. It was her chance to say what she had to say, what she needed to say, but that didn't make her feel any better. Now she didn't even think she could explain. Maybe she wasn't capable of explaining, after all.

The facts were just facts, but they didn't take in the basic fact in the whole mess, that she'd fallen in love with him.

She'd never say that. She'd never open herself up to this man that way. She'd just take whatever came and she'd leave. She took the steps slowly, going toward Jack. When she couldn't bear to be any closer, she stopped. There were three feet separating them.

He erased that space with one stride. He looked down at her for what seemed an eternity, then said, "We need to talk."

Something she would have jumped at until now almost horrified her. She shook her head and looked down. "No, we don't. You know all you need to know."

He stood there, silent, until she was forced to look up at him again. "No, I don't," he said.

"What more do you want?"

He closed his eyes for a moment, then his eyes met hers. "The truth."

"The truth? What are you going to do with that?" She was more than a bit surprised that her voice was steady.

He hunched his shoulders and rocked forward on the balls of his feet. "I don't know. But I deserve to hear the truth from you, don't you think?"

He was right. He did deserve it. She exhaled. "I went there to work. That was all. It's my job."

"And me? I was your job? Get close to me? Find out what you could?"

She hadn't tried to get close to him. That had just happened. But why bother to deny it? It was too late now. "It was a good idea. You're the best at what you do, and my client wanted to hit the ground running, not doing trial and error."

For some reason, as she spoke, he stepped back, building space again. His eyes narrowed. "And you did it well."

She shook her head. "No, I didn't. I got what they wanted, but I messed it all up."

He stared at her...hard. "Yes, you did mess it all up," he muttered. "I'd say you're the best at that."

She didn't want to do this. She wouldn't. "I need to get..." Where? She couldn't even come up with a lie, so she started again and meant what she said. "Well, have a good life. I hope you find what you're looking for."

Jack heard the words, and all the pain and uncertainty he'd lived with for the past few days came into sharp, penetrating focus. He'd left Silver Creek, not looking back, and by the time he'd realized where he was going, he'd accepted it. He'd arrived in San Francisco yesterday, had Malone find out where Jillian lived, and in the process, find out where her dad was being cared for.

He'd gone by her apartment and there'd been no answer. Then he'd found this place, and finally saw her dad. Johnny O'Shay had surprised him. He knew he'd been sick, but Jillian had never mentioned Alzheimer's. He'd seen Johnny, and he looked as if he could get up and walk away from his wheelchair. He looked as if he was as healthy as anyone. He'd thought that until he'd introduced himself and met those blue eyes. Blue. The color he'd given to his daughter, but there was nothing there. They'd looked at him, and Johnny had said, "Hello." Then…nothing.

He'd talked to him, told him about meeting Jillian, realizing that the words were for himself, not for a man who was a prisoner in a world he didn't share with anyone. Jack knew how that felt. Not in the same way, but being in your life and being alone. He'd laid out things with Jillian in order, and when he'd heard the sound in the hallway, he'd known why he'd come. Why he'd had to come. And he wasn't going to let Jillian walk away without doing what he had to do.

"What do you think I'm looking for?" he asked her.

Blue eyes met his, and they seemed overly bright in the duskiness of night around them. "I don't know," she said on a whisper. "Only you know what you need."

"I need you," he said without thinking. Without planning. Without even knowing he'd say it until the words were in the air between them.

She flinched almost as if he'd struck her, and he didn't miss the unsteadiness in her when she released a breath. "You…Malone…he said you'd left, and that you didn't want to even talk to me on the phone."

He *had* said that to Malone. "I did," he said. "I got the Porsche and took some clothes and left. I went to Las Vegas, and Cain was gone. He and his wife had taken her daughter back to Silver Creek to see her aunt. I called Josh, and he and his new wife are on their honeymoon, and Gordie…" He shrugged. "He's busy with broken legs and head bumps." Jack looked up and down the evening street. "Can we talk in the car?"

He knew she was going to refuse even before she opened her mouth. "No."

"Then can we walk?"

She made a vague motion with her hands. "I suppose."

He would have taken her by the arm if he'd had to, but he didn't. She ducked her head and started up the street. He fell in step by her, barely noticing the old, impressive homes that lined the way. Most had been renovated into offices and apartments, or places like the one where Johnny O'Shay lived. He felt her sleeve brush his arm, and he knew she wasn't about to say the first word. So, he waited until they came to an intersection and she stopped.

She stared straight ahead, obviously waiting for him to choose a direction. "Let's head downhill," he said, and stepped off the curb to cross the narrow street. She stayed by him, and he matched his stride to hers. When he finally spoke, it wasn't what he wanted to say. "You've lived here ten years?"

"I went to college at Berkeley and stayed. Then Dad got sick and he moved here. He'd lived there alone since my mother died, and he couldn't anymore."

"How long has he been sick?" he asked, wanting to know on one hand, but trying to fill up the space around them with words on the other hand.

She slowed her pace and he matched it. "Probably since my mother died, ten years ago, but I only noticed it when I went back to see him after college.

He seemed fine at first, then he forgot things, he didn't remember simple things, and he would just sit there." They crossed another street and walked past a narrow park. "He knew me back then," she said, her voice barely above a whisper and almost lost on the growing breeze.

His heart lurched at her words. They weren't said with self-pity. But he remembered her comment about carrying the world on her shoulders, that she never dared shrug. "When did that happen?"

"When he didn't know me?"

All he wanted to do was to circle her shoulders with his arm and pull her against his side. But he kept his hands in his jacket pockets. "Yes."

She looked up at the sky over them, dark and starless, then released a breath that sounded more like a shudder. "Three years ago at Christmas. I took him his gifts, and had Christmas dinner with him at the home. It was all arranged, and it seemed so nice. We were in the dining room of the house, and two other residents were there with family. If you blurred it all, it could have been a real holiday meal."

She stopped then, but didn't look at him. She stood on the sidewalk, her head down, and he could see her eyes were closed as if she was avoiding something. Then she looked up, and it was then he realized she was crying. Tears slipped down her cheeks, and she made no motion to wipe them away. "He looked at me and asked who I was. Just like that. He was…gone."

Jack didn't bother fighting his urge then. He reached out and drew her to him. He cradled her into his chest and stroked her hair. In that moment, he knew Jillian in a way he hadn't thought possible. Such knowledge had only happened one other time. When he'd made love to her.

Now he held her on a street in a city he hardly ever visited, surrounded by strangers and the coldness of night. Yet he knew her and he knew everything he had to know to face the truth.

She didn't shake or sob, she just rested in his arms, and he finally shifted his hands, gripped her shoulders and moved her back enough to look into her face. Tears stained her cheeks, and her lashes were spiked. She was beautiful. And he loved her.

"I don't need to know anything about why you did what you did, or why you didn't tell me anything at The Inn," he said. When she would have spoken, he hushed her. "No, let me talk."

She bit her lip and just stood there, letting him hold her.

"I'm going to tell you what I was going to say when I came back and you were gone. The things I didn't get a chance to say." He swallowed hard, a tightness in his chest as he opened himself up completely to this woman in front of him. He said words he'd never said before, and he meant every one of them. "Jillian, it doesn't matter about the past. Nothing matters, except now. Here."

She stayed very still. "But Malone said…"

"Malone meant well. He just overstepped his bounds. He'd thought from the first that there was something off about you, and when he found you in Housekeeping, that raised a red flag. Then the wine cellar, and that camera phone, the way you didn't act like the other women who came to The Inn." He could almost smile. "He said you were far too polite and too considerate."

There was no smile from her, just a shuddering intake of air. "I tried to…" She cut that off. "I'm so sorry for everything. I really am."

"Me, too," he said, and let her go. He couldn't be touching her now, not with what he had to say. "I know now why I'm here. Why I ended up driving into San Francisco, why I talked to your boss. I didn't like him at first. He's way too protective of you. Then he softened and he really talked you up. He's in your corner, big-time."

"Ray's a good man. He's not doing subversive things, or asking me to do them. It's all fact-finding. That's it."

"I know. I know. He made that clear. He also told me that you refused to do more work for the company that's after the land."

"I didn't want to be involved with whatever they did at Silver Creek," she said simply.

"Why? You need the job. Ray said you need the money, that you pay a fortune for your father's care."

"I just didn't want to," she said, her voice getting lower and lower. "He'll get me more work with other clients."

Jack gently framed her face with his hands, tipping her chin so she'd have to look at him. "Why couldn't you do it?"

She shook her head, breaking free of him. She

resumed walking, more quickly now, almost jogging. He went after her, got to her side and stayed there for four more blocks. They were so close to the bay now that he could see the lights reflecting off the dark surface of the water. "Why?" he persisted, and knew his whole world hung on her answer.

She kept quiet and didn't stop walking. She turned on the main street, heading away from a series of shops and toward a cleared area that looked like docks outlined in looped lights. She didn't stop until she couldn't go any farther. He stood by her on the sidewalk at the fence that kept the public from going into what looked like a marina. Boats bobbed in the dark water, and he could see that several looked as if people lived on them year-round.

He saw Jillian grip the metal cross rail of the fence, then she lowered her head and closed her eyes. He waited. The sound of boats drifted to them through the night air and occasionally people passed, talking and laughing. Life went on while Jack knew his life was in the balance. He finally spoke because he couldn't wait any longer.

"Jillian? Why wouldn't you go back to Silver Creek and help them get what they wanted?"

"I couldn't," she said, not looking at him. "I didn't want to be there. There was no reason to be there."

"If there was a reason, would you come back?"

She sighed heavily and finally turned to him. The security lights around the marina cast sharp shadows at her cheeks and throat. Her eyes were all but hidden in shadow. "I don't have a reason to go back. I turned down any follow-up job."

This was it. He had to either say what he came to say, or leave…alone. He braced himself, feeling more uncertainty than he could ever remember feeling. "Will you come back with me?"

She stared at him. "You're not going to be there."

"If you're there, I'll be there."

"I don't—"

"Jillian, I don't care what you did. I don't care what's happened before. The only thing about the past I care about is when I saw you at midnight and kissed you." The unsteadiness he heard in his voice unsettled him. "That's the smartest thing I've ever done."

She was silent, just watching him.

"I'm not sure how to say this. I've never said it before." He took a breath and hunched forward, as if preparing for a blow to the midsection. "I want you to come home with me. I want you to be with me. I want you to love me."

The night was around them, the world moving to its own rhythm, but neither one knew it existed right then. Jack waited. It was the hardest thing he'd ever had to endure, and when Jillian finally spoke, he felt everything fit into place. All the crazy oddities that he'd never understood before made sense, and it was all because of this woman.

"I do love you," she said simply.

He let the words settle in his soul, then he touched

her again. He framed her face with his hands again, felt her silky heat under his fingers and everything made sense. "I love you," he managed to say.

"But I'm not alone. There's Dad. I can't just—"

"Shh," he said softly. "I love everything about you, and your dad is part of our world."

He heard a soft gasp, then she stepped into his arms. Her face was buried in his chest, but he heard what she said with aching clarity. "I love you, I love you, I love you."

He closed his eyes tightly, just holding her, then he said, "Just be with me, wherever we are?"

"Anywhere you are," she breathed as she stood on tiptoe and found his lips with hers.

Home. Jack knew the meaning of that simple word. Wherever he was with Jillian would be home.

Epilogue

Valentine's Day

Jack hurried up to his suite, got out of the elevator and half ran through the outer room into the living area. He gazed around, but Jillian wasn't there. The sinking feeling in his stomach hit him as he called her name and no one answered.

He turned, intending to go back down and find her, but Malone walked in right then.

"Boss?" he said. "Got a message for you."

"Take care of it," Jack said. "I'm looking for Jillian. We were supposed to meet at six, and it's…" He checked his watch. "Six-ten."

"Wow, she's late, huh?"

The big man was actually smiling. No, his lips were lifting slightly, and Jack could have sworn it was the start of a smile. "Okay, ten minutes. I'll see you later. I'm going to go search for her."

"She's not with Johnny," Malone said as Jack got to the door to leave.

Jack pivoted. "What?"

"Just saw Johnny and he's doing fine. Doc said he's in pretty good shape, all things considered. Although he won't get better, he seems calm, and happy with his new accommodations."

That was a huge relief. They'd brought Johnny to Silver Creek a week ago, after Jack had arranged to have a room in their wing, but on the bottom floor, set up for his care. The new nurse was pleasant, understood what she was dealing with. And something in Jillian had eased when Johnny had finally arrived. She spent a lot of time with him, even though he didn't know who she was. But he smiled when she came in, and that was enough.

"Jillian was down there?"

Now he was certain Malone was smiling. "She was."

"What's the joke?"

"Nothing. I was just thinking that you're making me revisit my attitude about women and marriage."

"What?"

"You've been married what, a month?"

They'd married quietly at City Hall in San Francisco before they'd headed back here. "It's our anniversary today."

"Ah, Valentine's Day. Romantic. Real romantic."

The big man was enjoying this. "Yes, it is," Jack said. "Where is she?"

"Waiting for you."

"You knew all this time, and you—"

Malone held up a hand, then crossed to where Jack stood. "Hold on. I came to tell you, but you cut me off. Last time you did that, well…" He lifted his massive shoulders, and the action tested the fabric of his dark shirt. "Whatever. She told me to just say 'Spectacular' and you'd understand what she meant."

Jack understood exactly what she meant. He grabbed his jacket, then called over his shoulder as he hurried out, "Don't come hunting for me, no matter what. Okay?"

"Got it, boss," Malone said, and as Jack stepped into the elevator to ride down and the door started to shut, he thought he heard the big man chuckling.

When he stepped out on the ground floor he didn't look right or left as he put on his jacket and headed for the exit and his Porsche, parked at the foot of the stairs. He got in, brought the engine to life and roared off. He went out of the gates, and headed south. He barely noticed anything as he drove through Silver Creek. Then he saw his destination. She'd left the gates to the old estate open for him, and within two minutes he'd parked right next to her SUV by the stairs that led to the loft at the stables.

He got out of his car and ran up the stairs two at a time. Damn it, he was still running after the woman. He was smiling when he got to the door and reached for the knob. But Jillian opened the door before he touched the knob.

She stood in front of him in a simple red sleep shirt fashioned of silk, with ribbon shoulder straps. It fell to the middle of her thighs and clearly defined her high breasts. "Hello," he said. "Malone gave me your message."

"Spectacular," she said as she pulled him inside. "I always liked that giant. He is such a great messenger." As the door swung shut, she tugged Jack's jacket off in the hallway, then tossed it onto a chair before she took his hand and led the way to the loft.

It had changed since their first time here. Most of the furniture was gone, and in its place was one piece, a huge bed set at a perfect angle to see the world out the windows. She turned into his embrace, and he lifted her so she could wrap her legs around his hips as her arms circled his neck. "He's a real Renaissance man, don't you think?"

Jack kicked behind him to shut the door and walked slowly toward the bed with Jillian in his arms, the only light in the room coming from the fire she'd laid in the hearth. "I'm not here to talk about Malone," he whispered against her neck, his voice growing rougher as she kissed his forehead, then his jaw. He barely noticed that there were roses in a vase near the windows, or that the bedsheets were pulled down. He never even looked at the world outside. His world was in here with his wife.

He fell into the bed with her, and what he'd thought would be a leisurely coming together turned into a frantic need for each other. Her shirt was gone, and he got out of his clothes as quickly as he could. Then they were together in the linen, body against body, heat mingling. The heat grew, and she was over him. She was moving, and he felt her. He arched back, trying to be as deeply in her as possible, then he heard her cry out, and his voice joined hers.

He didn't let her go. He stayed in her as long as he could, then he finally rolled to one side, facing her. Her face was flushed, and her eyes soft with satisfaction in the flickering shadows. Her hand traced his jaw, then touched his lips. "I love you, Jack," she whispered. "I love you."

He kissed her quickly, then drew back. "Thank you," he found himself saying. And that encompassed so much. Thanks for loving him. Thanks for being with him. Thanks for making his life complete.

Jillian snuggled into him, and her scent filled him. As her hand wandered over his chest, she said, "I saw Dad, and I can't thank you enough for what you did."

"Oh, no, don't thank me. I'm totally selfish. I want you with me, and I want you to be happy. And I know that having Johnny here is a good thing for you."

She pressed her lips to his chest, then raised herself on an elbow to gaze down at him. Her hair tangled around her face, and her lips looked swollen from their kisses. "It's a good thing. This is all a good thing."

He brushed at her errant curls. "We can live wherever you want, wherever you feel is best. Your idea about taking over this place has its merits, but if we do that, we keep this room a secret. A huge lock on it, that only we have the keys for. It's ours."

"Oh, yes, that sounds wonderful." She glanced out

at the night and the world spread far below. "The world at our feet."

He kissed her and drew back. "That's better than on your shoulders."

She sobered and kissed him back. "I thank you for that, too, for letting me shrug and not have everything come crashing down."

He stroked her cheek. "We can do the house later."

"For now this is good. But you know, I love the idea of being where your great-great something-or-other built his wine cellar, and I love the idea of being in this town where you grew up, and I want to be where your close friends are. Mostly, though, I just want to be with you." She dipped her head to kiss his chest, then pressed a hand to his heart. "This is perfect."

"You don't mind living at The Inn until I get Malone ready to take it over?"

She hesitated, then shook her head. "Malone's a fast learner. And Duncan Bishop really seems to want the other land. It won't be developed. He and his wife will use it to make a family. And until everything settles down, I can wait and we can be at The Inn, until we need more space to…" She shrugged. "Just until we need more space."

He shifted to face her more squarely. "For what?"

"I was thinking, if, somewhere in the future, we happen to have a baby or two, we'll need a house and land and lots of space for the kids to play. This place will be perfect."

He stared at her. "Are you…?"

"Pregnant? Oh, no. I'm not. We haven't even talked about children. But if you want a child with me, this house would be great. Your folks don't want it, and I think I'd like it. We could even get horses again."

A child with Jillian? It hadn't crossed his mind until that moment. A child with Jillian. Yes, he'd like that…in a while. Maybe when his need to be with her wasn't a constant thing. Maybe when he could be away from her for a while and not feel as if he was dying.

Then she kissed him, and she laughed softly. "Don't look so serious. We'll talk…later."

She came to him again, and as he rolled to be over her, as he entered her, he knew that his need of her was forever. He'd never stop dying when they were apart. And they'd have a child, maybe two children. And they'd have a home.

Although he'd left Silver Creek for less than a week before they got back together, he felt as though he'd returned home after a long, long time. "I love you," he said, and couldn't wait to wake up with Jillian the next morning and the morning after that and…forever.

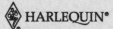
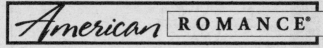

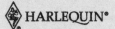

HARLEQUIN®

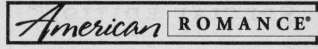

IS DELIGHTED TO BRING YOU FOUR NEW
BOOKS IN A MINISERIES BY POPULAR AUTHOR

Jacqueline Diamond

Downhome Doctors

First-rate doctors
in a town of second chances

A FAMILY AT LAST
On sale April 2006

Karen Lowell and Chris McRay fell in love in high
school, then everything fell apart their senior year
when Chris had to testify against Karen's brother—
his best friend—in a slaying. The fallout for everyone
concerned was deadly. Now Chris, a pediatrician, is
back in Downhome, and asking Karen for her help....

Also look for:

THE POLICE CHIEF'S LADY
On sale December 2005

NINE-MONTH SURPRISE
On sale February 2006

DAD BY DEFAULT
On sale June 2006

Available wherever Harlequin books are sold.

SPECIAL EDITION™

DON'T MISS THE FIRST BOOK IN

PATRICIA McLINN's

EXCITING NEW SERIES

Seasons in a Small Town

WHAT ARE FRIENDS FOR?

April 2006

When tech mogul Zeke Zeekowsky returned for his hometown's Lilac Festival, the former outsider expected a hero's welcome. Instead, his high school fling, policewoman Darcie Barrett, mistook him for a wanted man and handcuffed him! But the software king and the small-town girl were quick to make up....

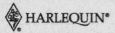
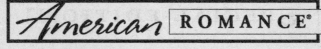
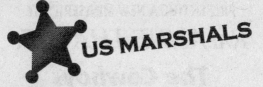